CW00798655

Dust In The Wind

Dust In The Wind

Nanncy J Steward

Library of Congress Control Number: 2022920675

ISBN:	Hardcover	978-1-6698-5442-5
	Softcover	978-1-6698-5441-8
	eBook	978-1-6698-5440-1

Print information available on the last page.

Rev. date: 11/07/2022

To order additional copies of this book, contact:
Xlibris
844-714-8691
www.Xlibris.com
Orders@Xlibris.com
845370

CONTENTS

Dedication

To my beloved Monster and Pooh whose unconditional love and devotion has gotten me through the best and the worst times. No one could ask for better familiars. And to all my other familiars waiting in the Summerland, I have not forgotten you…I'll hug you again one day. To my gingers Mango and Magic who brighten each and every day.

For you, Mom, you never truly believed in me. To you writing was a waste of time…now you can believe.

To those who have believed in me through the years, thank you; your words of encouragement meant the world to me. Thanks for making me laugh Danny!

And to my mentor, Cecil Neth, who made my days at Colorado State University special.

Incubus

In the pitch black
Of the witching hour
You whisper my name
Beckoning me from
My slumber
Your icy touch glides
Across my warm body
Like a welcome breeze
On a hot summer night
Urgently expressing
Your desires
My unearthly lover
Your breath, cold yet inviting
Tantalizes my senses
Your kiss endearing
But sweeps my breath away
I am drawn to your embrace
Like a moth to a flame
In the darkness
We are bound by
Our seductive dance
Of unbridled passion
Time seemly stands still
Within this preternatural universe
Moans of desire
Echo through the ebony night
As dawn peaks through
The crack in my blinds
I awaken cold, alone, spent
Your touch lingering
Along my thighs
Your scent still in the air
The taste of your kisses
Etched upon my lips I lay in dream-like state
Awaiting your return
In the witching hour.

Valley of Shadow

The world is a bleak tableau
And I, cast from the panoramic stage
Weep for all that has
Been robbed from my being
In one shattered moment
As array of dreams
Lay in shards beneath my feet
The blood runs cold in my veins
As the earth greedily enfolds
The sacrificial offerings
In icy hibernation.

All Hallows Eve

Wind blowing through the screen
Black cat howls
In the dead of night
Awakening the spirits
Who roams the realms
When the veil between
The land of the living
And the land of the dead thins
A ghostly melody floats upon the winds
As the underworld dandy
Dances through the tombstones
Flirting with the long departed
Souls of ages gone by
Exalted visions bound upon the terrestrial sphere
Witches weave spells in the darkest hours
Familiars watch swaying
To the beat of the ancient's chants
As the night comes to life with
The myths of the generations
Candles burn, flicker as the dead
Pass through the veil, then fade within the shadows
On their way to the Summerland
Magic is afoot
Wear a mask out into the night
To ward off evil that lurks
In the stillness of the darkness
Stay far away from the churchyard gate
At the midnight hour
Or you might become the cemetery walker
Honor all those gone before you
Whether they be beast or human
Light a candle of white
To guide them on their journey
All Hail All Hallows Eve

Life Everlasting

It was the year 1887. The cool, crisp autumn was filled with magic, just a hint of frost in the air. I was twenty three years old. The last harvest was upon us, a time my father had called Samhain. I felt invigorated for the first time since my father's death in the spring. My house keeper had been busy baking breads and the aroma of delectable dishes of the season filled the air.

"Tilley whatever will we do with all this food?" I said laughing.

"Sorry Miss," she said bowing her head. "It's a hard habit to break having done this for your family all these years."

"I know it's alright…really. What we don't eat I'll have sent down to the church."

"Will you be having dinner at midnight?"

"Yes. Father would be so disappointed if we didn't. Tilley curtsied and turned to stir a pot on the stove. "Tilley, be sure to dress up nice for dinner it'll just be me and you. We'll fill our plates here in the kitchen and eat at the grand table in the dining room."

"You want me to join you, Miss?" she said. "I thought Mr. Daniels would be joining you."

"No Tilley, he didn't even respond to my invite…" her voice trailed off.

"Ungrateful, unforgiving lot they are, Miss, after all your father had done for this community this is how they treat you."

"Yes, it appears I am to be shunned by the Sacred 36 and all within their circle because of the scandal." I wiped away a tear that rolled down my cheek. “Now Tilley will you be joining me for dinner?”

“Oh yes, Miss. It’s been a long time since I able to dress in one of my good dresses.” Tilley smiled as she bustled about the kitchen.

“Good. I can’t think of anyone I’d rather share dinner with. I think I’ll go to the parlor and read until it’s time to change into my gown.”

As the ancient clock in the corner chimed the 8 o’clock hour I went up the winding stairs to my room. I stopped at my father’s door, remembering how I would watch him as he fumbled with his tie as he got ready for a dinner party. It seemed long ago since he’d stood in this room, far longer than the six months since his death. I stepped into the room it was just the way he’d left it. I lovingly ran my hand along the velvet bedspread. I picked up his smoking jacket, holding it close as I inhaled deeply of his scent and the spicy scent of cloves. Tears filled my eyes as I ran down the hall to my room.

The 9 o’clock hour chimed as made my grand entrance down the stairs dressed in the latest fashion from Paris. My dress was low cut showing off my cleavage; it was made from red satin, covered in a black lace overskirt with tiny beads dangling off the hem. I wore my favorite leather boots that father had brought back from Italy two summers prior. My auburn hair was combed away from my face but left to flow freely down my back. As I descended the staircase I greeted my invisible guests with my most dazzling smile, nodding haughtily at the Denver high society. I thought of witty things to say with just enough sarcasm to make the comments sting.

I laughed walking about the room pretending I was still part of the sacred high society, lost in my fantasy. I sat before the fireplace in the great chair and sipped a rum and punch as my illusion faded enjoying the quiet solitude within the darkened walls of the stately mansion on Grant Street. My thoughts turned to the weeks before my father’s death. He’d died amongst rumors of witchcraft and hedonistic rites being performed within our gardenwalls; his character tarnished, leaving me alone and shunned by everyone. A nosy passerby had heard him chanting in the garden and had climbed the wall to see my father naked performing a ritual one full moon night. The rumors flew through the city like a wildfire catches in dry tinder, unstoppable until it runs out of fuel.

Denver society suddenly turned their back on one of their most beloved professors, the university said they'd no longer needed his consults and the students he tutored left his service one by one. Father never let on the rumors of devil worship bother him he walked down the streets with his head held high and greeted everyone as he always had. But the lack of visitors to the house, the loose of his friends took its toll. He busied himself with his studies, started to write his epic novel when he caught a cold. The cold lingered for weeks, finally turning into pneumonia. My father died late one spring night with me and Tilley by his side; neither his friends nor colleagues came to his funeral. We buried him on a cold, over cast morning in the cemetery on the hill. Tilley and I walked with the hearse to his grave as people we had called friend turned away as we passed by. For weeks after I buried myself within the walls of our home afraid of what I might hear when I walked down the streets. No one came by to see how I fared or if I needed anything. I had never felt so alone in my life.

I had never followed the teachings of my father very well nor had I paid much heed to the Christian teachings my mother had taught me. Father had said that someday I would find my calling. As I sat alone in my empty home I felt abandoned by both father's Goddess and mother's God, lost in a sea of nothingness. I sat watching the flames dance upon the logs intertwining like impassioned lovers. I poured another rum and punch from the pitcher that Tilley had left on the table before she went to dress for our grand meal. I smiled sadly brushing away the tears that seemed to flow from nowhere. I sipped my drink as father's teachings about Samhain suddenly flowed through my mind. I began to pace about the room hearing his words.

"Child, it is one the most spiritual Sabbats, when the veil between the living and the dead is at its thinnest point. Always remember to honor those who have passed on in this night."

I ran to the door grabbing my cloak, calling to Tilley I'd be back soon. The full moon hung low over the tree tops, a magnificent glowing orb in the sky. A chilly autumn wind began to blow caressing the trees lining the streets of Denver, whispering secrets on the night air. The leaves rustled under my skirts as I hurried to the cemetery hoping to catch a glimpse of my father one more time. As I neared the cemetery I slowed my pace that curious nervous, scared and excited feeling rose from the pit of my stomach. I took several deep breaths and stopped in the shadows next to the cemetery gates. Suddenly I was afraid to enter the graveyard, an owl hooted from the limb of the cottonwood bough high above me. I stood deathly still watching the sea of tombstones before me. Time stood still as I kept my vigil; I had no idea how long I stood there like a statute keeping vigil.

I had the odd sensation of being watched, a twig snapped in the distance and I bolted from the shadows. I ran up the street as if the dead were racing after me until I was out breath, my corset binding, but I continued to walk briskly towards home, greedily gulping in the night air. I was still several blocks from home as the sound of music drifted upon the wind, I followed its melody, mesmerized by its rhythm. I found myself on the garden patio of the Hill mansion peering into the ballroom. Inside a gala was being held for a visiting Viscount from Europe. An orchestra played a lively waltz as couples danced under the crystal chandeliers, laughing, swirling in time to the music. I closed my eyes, lost all track of time as my body swayed to the rhythm of the music. Once again, I had the feeling of someone watching me. I opened my eyes and looked about the ballroom when I saw him watching from across the room, his eyes beckoning me.

He was tall, with shoulder length hair, black as coal with a touch of silver at the temples, his skin was the color of ivory.

He smiled disarmingly and raised his glass of champagne to me as he motioned for me to come in. My heart raced, I stumbled backwards, knocking over a flower pot in my haste to get away. As I ran up the steps to my front door I stopped, slowly turning, looking back up the street. I was sure someone had followed me, though I saw no one, I could not shake the feeling. As I opened the front door, the clock began to strike the midnight hour, I slammed the door shut, locking it as I peered out into the street.

"The midnight hour is upon, Miss," Tilley called as she began to light the candles about the formal dining room.

"I'm coming, Tilley." I said still trying to catch my breath. I threw my cape over the chair and glanced back to the door making sure it was locked. I entered the dining room, smiling lovingly at Tilley. She had placed photos of my father, my mother and her late husband at the table. As Tilley poured us a glass of wine I walked to the window and peered out into the night, I could feel hungry, greedy eyes watching from the darkness.

In the days that followed the city buzzed with gossip about the gala at the Hill mansion and the eccentric viscount, Roger Saint James. Tilley returned from shopping with the latest gossip.

"They say he sleeps the day away; he's never seen before dusk and stays up all night carousing. He fancies himself quite the ladies' man, a different woman on his arm every night," she lowered her voice to a whisper. "They say he's been seen leaving the red-light district several nights in a row with one of those crib girls hanging on him."

"Oh, no," I laughed, feigning shock.

"Don't make light, Miss. This one's a rogue for sure."

"And what if he is, Tilley? Who are we to judge after the way the good folks of this town have judged us?"

"Sorry, Miss…I just got caught up in the gossip, the excitement."

"I know. I just do not want to hear the talk from these hypocritical fools."

"Miss, I did not mean to upset you…"

"Tilley, I know that. And I am sorry you have had to deal with the gossip about my father. It hasn't been easy for you either."

"Do not worry your pretty head over that, Miss. I still have my friends and they do not judge like those high society folks." She smiled as she put the groceries away.

The days were growing colder, there was a hint of snow in the air, and a rainbow had encompassed the moon the evening before, a sure sign. I was as restless as my grey stallion pawing and snorting at his paddock. I pulled the pins from my long auburn locks letting them fall freely about my waist. I put on my riding skirt and coat and pulled on my riding boots. I ran to the stable feeling wild and carefree; Poco raised his head, nickering when he saw me. I quickly fastened the leather bridle about his head and swung onto his sleek back. I scandalously straddled my horse like a man, riding through the streets, laughing at the mock horror on the faces of Denver's finest as they whispered about my unseemly behavior. I headed Poco out onto the open plains east of town, giving him his head, we ran like the wind, the warm autumn sun upon our backs. As the afternoon sun began to wane I headed Poco back towards the city. By the time we rounded the corner into our neighborhood the chilly evening wind was starting to kick up, lamps and candles were being lit in the homes that lined the streets. A paper blew across the street in front of us, Poco snorted and side stepped away from it. I reined him in and stroked his massive neck, talking to him, softly.

"Many a man would have been unseated by that," a British accent floated on the wind. "You are an excellent horsewoman," he added.

"Thank you," I said, still quieting my horse.

He walked out of the shadows taking hold of Poco's reigns. "I meant that every bit a compliment. I am Viscount Roger Saint James." He removed his hat and bowed his head ever so slightly.

I smiled. I could not help myself; he was bit as charming as I had heard. "I am Lacey Templeton," I said offering my hand. He gallantly kissed my leather glove.

"Why did you not come into my party the other night when I beckoned to you?"

I smiled I was not used to someone being so blunt in this town. "Viscount, I am no longer invited to those parties."

He smiled back, his ice blue eyes penetrating my very soul. "So I'm told. We will have to see what we can do about that."

I laughed trying to kick Poco on but he would not release the reigns. "May I call on you, Miss Templeton?

I paused looking into his beautiful eyes, my breath catching in my throat. "Yes," I replied, "Yes, you may."

"Good. I will call tomorrow eve around seven." He smiled that radiant, heart-breaking smile and he was gone. I rode home wondering if the conversation had been real or just in my head.

The next night the door ringer sounded promptly at 7 o'clock as the grandfather clock struck the hour. Roger Saint James sat in my parlor patiently waiting to call on me. I wanted to rush down the stairs to greet him but Tilley said it not lady like and made me wait nearly half an hour before she allowed me to head down the stairs. I entered the parlor, offering my hand to the Viscount. He kissed my hand and I swooned, his presence made me giddy and tongue tied like a school girl. He had brought me a small bouquet of flowers which I gave to Tilley to put in water. I dismissed her for the evening and offered the Viscount a seat in the parlor. We talked and laughed easily. As the night grew late he asked if I wanted to go for a walk in the cold night air, he instructed his servant to follow us in the carriage. He offered his arm to me, I smiled as we walked down the streets, it felt as if this was my destiny to walk beside this mysterious foreigner. It seemed as if we walked about for hours, talking about everything under the sun. It was well after midnight and I shivered as the wind grew colder. We rode back in the carriage exchanging smiles as Roger leaned over and stole a kiss from me. He asked me to join him after dinner the next night. We sat in my parlor talking, laughing and exchanging kisses until almost dawn. I went to bed as the sun rose in the eastern sky, dreaming of Roger St James, my stomach full of butterflies with thoughts of our kisses. We were to become constant companions from that night on.

Roger decided to take up residence in several rooms he rented on Holladay Street just off the bawdy red-light district. He said he liked his privacy and no self-respecting member of Denver society would want to be seen on Halladay Street. Throughout the remainder of the fall, the winter and into the spring I accompanied him to every party he was invited to. Denver society was scandalized to have me among them once again. Anyone who dared to refuse me into their homes or was over-heard saying anything unkind was noted in his man servants book to be forever held in the Viscount's disfavor.

With each party I became more and more confident, I expressed my views on the Dawes Act and women's rights. I was well read, quoted from Shakespeare and Robert Louis Stephenson. Roger swelled with pride as I grew out of my shy, reclusive ways. I saw him smile and turn away to keep from laughing as bested many a high society know it all with my knowledge of current affairs.

Shortly after the holidays our relationship became more serious. The night was frigid, the wind howling, as the first snow of the new year began to fall. Roger suggested we stay in, he had grown weary of the endless parties and wanted to spend some time with me alone. As usual he toyed with his food and sipped from one of the bottles of wine he always brought with him. After dinner we settled back before the fireplace snuggling lazily in each other's arms. I was happier than I'd ever been. I was in love with Roger Saint James.

As the night wore on his kisses grew more intense, more urgent, his hands roaming freely about my body. We wound up in my bed chamber. His fingers nimbly undoing the buttons on my dress, he threw my clothes about the room with carless abandon. He pushed me back unto the bed, kissing me hard, then pulled away looking deep into my eyes.

"I have something to tell, love," his voice was husky with desire. "You have stirred something inside me I cannot control."

I reached playfully for his neck, trying to kiss him. He grabbed my hands tightly, pinning them over my head and kissed me long and hard taking my breath away. I felt the urgency of his manhood.

"Lacey...Lacey, I am a vampire." His stare was intent, I thought his blue eyes would penetrate to my very soul.

I gasped. "So that is why no one ever see's you in the light of day..." I squealed with delight, like a young girl. "I love you, Roger." I pulled him closer, baring my neck. He smiled and bared his fangs but his lips brushed past my neck to my breast as his razor-sharp teeth cut deep within me, moaning with ecstasy as he sucked my life force. I felt his manhood enter me and take my purity, I belonged to Roger Saint James in every sense of the word. Throughout the long winter nights I writhered under his weight, like a wanton, joyously making love to my knight of the darkness.

Winter turned into spring; the flowers began to peek out from their hibernation along the foothills of the Rocky Mountains. Summer came and Roger announce he had eyes for no one but me and intended to marry me. Denver society was once again buzzing with gossip. By the end of the summer of 1888 I became ill, Roger never left my side. The doctors said they could find nothing wrong with me, yet I was growing weaker by the day. Both Roger and I knew it was his nightly feeding on me. He said it was time for me to make some decisions, to put my affairs in order.

"Are you sure this is what you want?' he asked one more time.

"More than anything, my love, need you ask?" I coughed, gasping for breath. "How long do I have?"

"You decide when you want me to turn you." He tried to smile, visibly shaken by my weakened state. "but don't wait too long...I cannot bear to see you in so much pain."

I took his hand in mine, caressing his long fingers admiring his ring of garnet and onyx, as I always had. "I want to arise on

Samhain night," I said, smiling the most radiant smile I could muster. Roger kissed me gently, pulling me into his arms.

Over the next few weeks I began to put my affairs in order. I made arrangements for Tilley to live in the mansion, I left enough money for her to live out her life in comfort and at her death my home was to be placed in the hands of a caretaker; some lost 'niece' of mine would come to claim my home in the future. I wired my money to accounts in New York City under several aliases. I had what belongings I could not bear to part with packed and shipped back east. I gave my stallion to Roger to care for until he turned me. Lastly I purchased a coffin, picked out my tombstone and made arrangements to be buried in the family plot.

Tilley doted over me, never giving up hope I'd get well. She had watched her husband die, my mother, my father and now me. I could not offer any words of comfort. I was dying and whether I let Roger make me a vampire or not, I would soon be dead. At last October 30th came, Roger arrived just after dusk. He looked sad but at the same time an air of excitement lay just below the surface. I had been awake since dawn; I was exhausted but I had not wanted to miss one moment of my last day as a living creature.

The evening hours ticked by slowly as I instructed Roger to lay out my best riding outfit and boots for me to be buried in. I gave him the letters I'd written to my father's lawyer and Tilley. Tilley came to my bedside one last time, her eyes were red from crying. I wanted to tell her everything, but Roger flashed a stern look my way and I bit my tongue.

I ran my finger tips lovingly along her soft cheek as she sat beside me and held her hand. "Tilley, never forget that I love you…I appreciate your loyalty as much as my father did." She began to cry. "Shhh, my friend. It's alright, it is not the end it is just the close of one chapter and the beginning of another."

"I know, Miss," she sobbed. "I just never thought you would join your father in your prime."

"Nor I, Tilley," I looked to Roger and smiled sadly. "Now promise me you'll take of yourself."

"I will, Miss Lacey." She began to cry harder.

"Tilley, light a white candle at dark tomorrow night and place it in the parlor window to light the way for the dead on our journey." Tilley squeezed my hand and kissed me on the cheek, she rose and walked to the door and turned to look at me one last time before she ran down the hallway.

Roger closed the door, locked it and turned to me. "I have instructed my servant to be hereat sunrise to carry out your instructions to be buried in the morning. I will instruct him to tell everyone that I will not be at the graveside service as I cannot bring myself to watch you lowered into the dark, cold earth. I will make my appearances around town tomorrow night and say my good-byes to Denver before you arise."

I looked around my room memorizing every detail, it would be a very long time before I would return to my home. Roger sat on the bed beside me and pulled me into his arms. "Are you ready, my love?" I smiled lovingly at him and nodded my head. He held me tightly as I felt his fangs pierce deeply into my vein. He drained me nearly to the point of death then punctured the vein in his wrist and held it to my lips. I drank greedily until he pushed me away.

I lay as if paralyzed watching him wipe the blood away from my mouth and neck, he dressed me in a fresh gown and changed the bedding. He threw it all it all in the fireplace watching the flames engulf the last moments of my life. As the gray light of dawn began to spill over the eastern horizon he hurriedly wrote a note to Tilley that I had died in the wee hours of the morning. As he put the note on the table by my bed he turned to me and smiled as he kissed me. "Sleep. I'll be waiting at the stroke of midnight."

The moon hovered high and bright in the dark sky on Samhain night as I awakened from my slumber. I walked from my grave, dusting the dirt off of my skirt. Out of the corner of my eye I caught the glimpse of a shadowy figure heading towards me, his hand raised in greeting. The breath caught in my throat, I waved back and he was gone. "Father," I called, "Father wait." But he had already slipped behind the veil of the dead and I was the undead, belonging to neither the world of dead or the living. Roger whistled to me from the hill where he waited with his fiery stallion and Poco. I ran to him, he wrapped a velvet cloak about my shoulders and kissed me long and hard, his lips warm and plump from feeding. He handed me the reins.

"Hurry, we have a long ride ahead of us before we catch up to my servant and you will need to feed soon." I smiled, listening and seeing the world for the first time as a vampire. I mounted Poco quickly, as Roger swung up onto his saddle with ease.

He leaned over gently talking my left hand in his. "One more thing…" he said placing a delicate ring of garnet and onyx on my finger. "To life everlasting my heart."

My senses were reeling wildly. To be born a vampire on this night and my maker declaring his undying love for me was more than I had ever dared to dream. I smiled radiantly at him, lovingly caressing the ring. "To life everlasting my love." We headed our horses out of town towards the plains and raced like the wind into the night.

Winter Masque

She hurries to the clearing
Where the Yule bonfires blaze
To watch from the shadows
Her breath catches in her throat
At the site of the Holly King
Bowing to the Goddess of Cold and Darkness
He is dressed in his finest red velvet
A sprig of holly adorning
His tangled white hair
The Queen smiles and pulls her
White furs about her as she settles
Back to watch the winter battle
One of the stags paws impatiently
At the crusted snow and snorts
As the nimble Oak King begins to taunt
The again King
The battle begins, rages
Breaks the stillness of the night
As the Holly King stumbles and fall
She rushes to his side
Tears run down her cheeks
As the revelers cheer on the new King
Her forgotten until the battle at Mid-Summer
When once again he rises to reign
In the quiet of their lodgings
She cares for him
Whispers tales of the greatness
And gently pulls blankets of fur
Over his tired body
She runs a hand lovingly
Across his broad chest and smiles
He smiles in return, winks
She crosses to the center of the room
And begins to dance slowly, seductively
To some ancient tune etched in her brain
As the holly King drifts
Into a long deep slumber.

Hauntings

I am the warrior princess
Whose spirit you have
Tortured throughout time
I would have followed you
To the depths
Of my broken, cold, black heart
But you have forsaken
My love for the quest
Of some forgotten dream
Leaving me unaccompanied
A warrior fallen by the wayside
I await your return
Like a cold, silent statue of alabaster
Tears glisten upon my cheeks
While visions of your conquests
Fill my waking hours
And haunt my slumber
I dream of your sensuous caress
Setting my every emotion on fire
The flame dancing, growing
As you wrap your inviting arms
Around me in ravenous embrace
Before the blood
In my veins turns to ice

Narcissus

Clouds bounding upon
    Myriads
Of golden dreams
    Past
Hover along the sparkling oceans
    Of
The sapphire universe
    Mythical
Etchings fade beneath
    The
Sun beams sinking
    On
The wings of a velvet songbird
    A
Flute echoes hauntingly
    Through
The hallow canyons
    Once
    Roamed by the Nymph
    As
    Narcissus watches reflecting
    Images
In the pool

And me thinks of days
When daffodils bloomed.

Solstice Dreams

Morning dawned; a fresh coat of snow glistened on the forest floor like a great white blanket tucking itself into every nook and cranny. Jack Frost had painted his signature lacy design across the landscape. The gray and barren trees shivered beneath his handy work but the holly and evergreens stood proudly beneath his icy blue artistry, gently swaying to the festive tune the winds carried.

The creatures of the forest slowly awoke within their warm, snuggly homes. The air tingled with the excitement of the season. It was time to decorate the great tree in the clearing for the Yule celebration. Everyone scampered about, some gathering food for the great feast, others rounding up decorations for the tree, others tending to the unruly youngsters, who could not contain their excitement. The forest came alive; everyone from the great bear down to the tiniest mouse had a task to perform. This was the one time of the year that all creatures of the forest put aside their differences.

A young mother fox looked on hungrily, drooling as a small army of mice marched on to the clearing carrying the buttons and bows they had been hoarding for months. playing in the snow, oblivious to everything but their playtime. Her stomach protested with an angry growl but she put thoughts of hunger aside, knowing that all would be rewarded at the festival with warm, creamy cereals, roasted nuts and roots, sweet treats and the delectable mead made by the fairy folk. Her mouth watered at the thought. She swatted one of her kits playfully on the bottom, watching it roll in the snow.

Even the miserly, beady-eyed rats made ready to contribute the candles that would illuminate the great tree. Through the year they had stolen candles from the neighboring farm houses saving them for this night. They snickered sarcastically to one and other, thinking about the delighted screams from young and old that would fill the forest air as the candles were lit one by one. Deep down they gloated over their very important role in the celebration.

Everyone scampered about except for one small rabbit named Bilbo. Bilbo stood at the window of his tiny cottage watching the creatures of the forest make ready for Yule. He paced nervously, in front of the fireplace fretting about his performance at the festival. He rehearsed his annual Yule litany over and over. He knew it by heart from years and years of reciting his legendary tale of the Holly King and his rival the Oak King. He knew when to pause for effect, knew when to raise his voice and when to lower it to make the unruly partiers strain to hear his musings; he knew how to convey happiness, sadness and fright with the slightest inflection in his voice. He practiced his songs and stories on Ranold watching his expressions and body language until he had the desired effect.

Bilbo was a revered member of the forest community. He had become the Bard of the Forest early in his years, because of an injury when he was caught in a hunter's trap. He had lain in the trap until the Fairy folk had found him and nursed him back to health. During his recovery they discovered his insatiable thirst for knowledge and began to recite the legends of yore for him to memorize and re-tell at the appropriate festivals as the wheel of the year turned.

The little poet took his duties as Bard of the Forest very seriously, traveling far and wide telling the legends of the ancients. He composed a ballad for every great deed done by Fairy and animal alike throughout his travels. Wherever he went he was made welcome and treated with respect. His skills as a Bard had become as legendary as the mythology he recited. He worried over tonight's oratory, wanted to be sure he might pique the interest of one the younger forest revelers who he might want to take under his wing as an apprentice bard. He was getting older and the constant travel was beginning to tell on his weary bones, it would be a comfort to know there would be someone to take over for him someday. He thought back to that very first festival he had sang and recited the stories, he'd been so scared but when the Fey and animal kingdom alike applauded and asked for more he knew he was meant to be the Bard.

Bilbo sighed and looked at his pocket watch he limped to the trunk at the foot of his bed and lovingly pulled his finest tuxedo and silk top hat out, laying it on the bed. He noticed a couple worn spots on the sleeves but determined it was good for one more festival. He dug deeper into the trunk for his best shirt and red and green ascot. He called to Ranold to brush out the wrinkles and bring him a cup of tea. He wanted nothing more than to take a nap having slept little the night before. He settled back into his favorite chair by the fireplace, closing his eyes so he'd be rested for the festivities.

As Bilbo slept the animals continued the preparations in the clearing. Each one brought a decoration for the tree and with the help of the birds even the highest limb came alive with festive ribbons and berries and finally the cherished candles were set in place. It was a steady stream of bodies going back and forth to the clearing all afternoon bringing presents to place around the great tree, tables were placed around the bonfires that were being built, wood was chopped and stacked, enough to keep the fires blazing until dawn. The Fairies would bring the special Yule log to light the fire and all would take a piece of it home to their hearths for luck throughout the year at the end of the festival. The food was brought and placed on the tables, berries, nuts, breads; the Fairies brought the sweet treats and kegs of mead. They erected the giant cauldrons over the fires so the creamy cereals could simmer and wrapped the roasted vegetable roots in clothes placing them near the fires to warm until the fest. It would soon be time for the Yule Sabbat to begin.

Bilbo awoke from his slumber, he shivered, it was cold in his tiny cottage. Ranold had let the fire burn out and was just placing a new log into the fireplace. Bilbo rose slowly, his bones protesting the cold draft and went to the hearth to take something from the tin he stored there. Ranold smiled as Bilbo placed a small piece of last year's log on the kindling. Bilbo watched as the wood sparked and the flame caught hold of tiny piece of wood. They clapped their tiny paws as the fire soon roared in the fireplace enjoying the warmth beginning to flow about the room.

He limped to the bed to begin dressing for the affair. His coat fit a little snugger than the last time he'd worn it, "too much feasting at the last sabbat," he whispered to himself, then giggled at a memory from that night. Ranold pinned a freshly picked sprig of holly with its berries to his lapel.

"Make sure the fire is secure until we return, Ranold. Now go enjoy the festival, eat, drink and be merry, my old friend," Bilbo said as he placed the top hat on his head, thumping the brim for luck. His limp was a little more pronounced than usual with the cold night air creeping into his old bones. He grabbed his favorite walking cane to aid his steps along the snowy path.

The bonfires set the whole clearing awash with light. Bilbo paused to take in the sight of all the forest inhabitants celebrating, merrily together. The Fairies had set their great table in the center of the clearing, they sat laughing and drinking. He breathed deeply of the aroma of the food cooking on the fire, a small stage had been erected, the great tree with its shimmering lights its backdrop, Bilbo clapped his paws with delight. He walked regally through the revelers, a hush fell over the crowd as he mounted the stage, as all eyes were upon him. He walked to the center of the stage and bowed. He reached for his tiny mandolin and began singing songs of the season. He paid homage to the Fairy kings and Queens of yore as well as the heroes of the forest. He invited everyone to sing along with the silly, festive songs of the season. After half an hour of filling the crisp night air with song he put down the mandolin and motioned for Ranold to bring him a cup of mead to wet his parched throat. He walked around the stage, watching the merry makers, gauging the moment to begin, he cleared his throat and in the most forceful voice he could muster began his oratory.

"Listen all ye creatures great and small who have gathered here tonight. Listen to the tale I am about tell..." Bilbo paused, waiting for the nosy youngsters to settle down before he continued.

"I am the Bard of the Forest, the keeper of the legends of yore. I have come tonight to tell you the story of the Great Holly King and The Oak King. There is a story as old as time. Long have they been bitter rivals, their dislike for each other so great that they come together twice a year and battle to the death of one opponent. Yes, they are bitter rivals but they know one cannot survive without the other and they play out their roles gallantly. At Yule the Holly King falls to the sword of the young Oak King but he will rise again and at the Mid-summer festival will do battle with his enemy again, this time he will emerge the victor. Some say they battle for the hand of the Goddess, yet she shows no favor to either one of them because she too knows that neither could exist without the other." He looked to the elder Fairies as they nodded their heads in agreement. He smiled to himself and held his hands above his head dramatically pausing ever so slightly before he began to paint images through his words.

"Hark! What is that I hear in the distance? Are those sleigh bells I here coming this way?" Everyone grew silent listening into night for the sound of sleigh bells. Behind the tree Ranold instructed the bears to shake a string of bells for effect. "Behold, The Holly King as he enters the battlefield in a sleigh pulled by eight magnificent stags, their harnesses made form the finest leather adorned with brass bells to ward off any evil that might be lurking in their path. They snort and paw at the ground impatiently as the King reins them in. His loyal subjects cheer their old King as he steps down from the sleigh. He is dressed in his finest red velvet suit, the cloth imported from the East especially for today. He bows to the crowd gathered to watch the battle. He rises and pulls his sword from its His tangled, long gray hair flows freely beneath his red hat. He has had a fresh sprig of holly sewn onto it sheath, the finely polished steel flashes in the light, a signal to the Oak King he is ready to fight.

The Oak King suddenly jumps nimbly from his perch high in the oak tree, grinning mocking the old King. He is young and viral, more than ready to take his place as the favored King. His long dark hair is tied back in a ponytail with a piece of leather. He is dressed in green with accents of gold, bronze and orange woven into his shirt and trousers. He cockily throws a ball of mistletoe at Holly King's feet, accepting the challenge. They lunge at each other as the battle begins. Swords flash, crash and clang, the sounds of battle echo through the forest." Bilbo paused. "If you listen very closely you can still hear the sound of the mighty swords clanging together on the night air. You can feel the frustrations of the Holly King as the Oak King taunts him and leads him into exhaustion. Still the battle rages on for hours.

The Fairy consorts of the Kings watch from the shadows as they fight. One knowing she will follow her King home in defeat, the other to bask in the light of the victor. The Holly Fairy worries about her Lord, sees him growing weaker with each blow, sees the fatigue in his face, it will soon be over and she will be caring for his wounds until he heals for the next battle. She frets, she paces knowing there is nothing she can do but watch. She wrings her hands in desperation listening to battle cries.

Swords clash one more time and the Holly King falls. The young Oak King moves in swiftly, driving his blade home as the Old king gasps in pain and falls in a heap. The Oak King raises his sword in victory as the crowd begins to cheer. The Oak Fairy rushes to his side, kissing him deeply on the lips. The revelers cheer, welcoming their new King.

The Holly Fairy run to her Lord and falls to her knees beside him. She holds his hand comforting him as best she can. She orders her servants to load him into the sleigh and begin the long trip home where she will tend to his wounds and give him a potion to sleep long and hard until tonight is just a memory. One last glance at the revelers she smiles sadly at her sister, the Oak King's consort and nods. She wipes the tears from her eyes and takes her place in the sleigh beside the Holly King. She pulls a warm fur blanket tightly about him, whispering calming endearments as they head home for a long winter's nap."

Bilbo paused, looked about the revelers listening intently. He held a paw up to his lips, "Shhhhhhh, if you listen very carefully on the wind you can still hear the sleigh bells as they fade into the night air." He held his paw up to his ear and turned his head to listen. The crowd sat spellbound listening for the sound of the sleigh bells.

Bilbo moved to the edge of the stage. "Now, my friends it is time to feast, to honor the Old King's passing and welcome the new King's reign. Join me in this celebration of love, peace until the dawn when the sun is reborn." Bilbo bowed; the revelers cheered as he left the stage.

Bilbo shook hands with those who were moved by his tale, excepting praise for his presentation. He took his place at the table with the Fairy royalty as a small band of traveling minstrels began to play a festive jig. A great platter of food and a goblet of the fairy mead was placed before him, Bilbo smiled at the generous portions, he was indeed famished. Before he could lift his goblet in toast a beautiful dark-haired Fairy Princess stepped forward kneeling before the small bard.

"Your Lordship, a small gift of our appreciation. You more than fulfill your duties as Bard of the Forest. Bilbo, this is for you." She smiled sweetly and moved away so all could see.

Bilbo carefully un-wrapped the brightly decorated package he pulled off the lid revealing a new tuxedo and silk top hat. He proudly held them up for all to see. Tears ran down his furry cheeks as he looked upon his gift, with a tiny paw he lovingly traced the outline of the collar of his new suit. At last, he looked up and thanked the Fairies. He rose from his chair holding the goblet of mead before him. "Creatures great and small join me in a toast on this night of love, hope and re-birth." He drank deeply from his goblet, settling back into his chair to watch the dancing and merry revelry through the night and the dawning of the sun.

Island Universe

In my island universe
I lie
Beckoning you to my side
Come be with me
My love

Travel to the tabloids
Of the unknown
Masters who once roamed
This fertile plain
Before our time
Searching the stars
Dreaming untold secrets
Deep within their minds

Come lie beside me
My love
And behold the dreams
Hidden in the stars of
Island universe

Unbound

Night wind blows
Gently caressing
Silent touches
Full moon glides
Across the velvet ocean
Of darkness
Small fairies drift
In flight through the glen
Flirting with fireflies
Draped in a silver
Blanket of sparkling dew
The forest shimmers
Beneath the glow from above
Slowly the moon drifts behind
A blanket of billowy clouds
Leaving a nocturnal sea
Of Shadow

Night Moves

On a bed of silken sheets
Surrounded by the sea of night
Impassioned lovers embrace
Speaking words of love
Wrestling as one
'Til the grey light of dawn
Find them
Entwined in each other's arms
Sleeping peacefully as two young babes

Starry, Starry Night

The bitter winds howled, blowing the deep, powder like snow into the forest, turning it into a desolate winter wonderland. The snows had changed from the gentle, whimsical storms at Yule into raging blizzards. The creatures of the forest huddled within their homes waiting for Imbolg when the first flowers sprung through the snowy tundra and the badger would stick his head out to predict how much longer the snows would come.

Bilbo paced restlessly in front of the window of his tiny cottage, the cold inched its way under the door and through every tiny crack and crevice. He fretted over the dwindling provisions in the pantry knowing they wouldn't last until spring. He had ordered his servant, Ranold to cut their daily rations in half hoping to make what food they had last a little longer. He also, told him to have only one fire going in the house at a time as the wood pile was growing steadily smaller with the bitter cold. In the mornings they would spend their time in front of the fireplace in the kitchen while Ranold prepared the daily meal, the fire would be allowed to burn out as the morning progressed and the fireplace in Bilbo's bedroom would be lit. The room was large enough to fit them both comfortably the rest of the day and night. Ranold had made a make shift bed at the foot of Bilbo's bed in front of the fireplace.

The Wolf Moon was drawing near and Bilbo could feel another storm approaching in his aching bones. Late at night he listened to the wolves howling their lonely, hungry song for all to hear. Just before the last storm Bilbo had sent a message with the Great Horned Owl to the Fairies that the forest creatures would soon be in trouble because of this hard winter. It was nearly two weeks since the owl had gone and he was worried the old coot had not been able to get to the Fae with the harsh winds. But in spite of his worries he instructed Ranold to pack a small bag of his belongings, he packed a bag of clothes and filled another with his journals and important books and placed it alongside Ranold's by the front door.

With one last worrisome look out into the frozen landscape Bilbo limped to his warm bedroom where he found Ranold happily lost in an old book. He crawled into bed and tried to read but his weary eyes grew heavy, and he was soon fast asleep. The weeks of worry were taking their toll on the tiny Bard.

Ranold and Bilbo woke with a start, the fire had burned out and a single candle illuminated the room. The loud pounding from the front room came again as Bilbo rose from his bed. "Stay where you are, Sir. I'll get it." Ranold grabbed his robe and ran into the freezing outer room, stubbing his toe on the way. Bilbo could hear him let out a string of oaths as he answered the door.

Two strangers dressed in long woolen cloaks with the hoods pulled low over their faces stood on the porch. "Forgive the late hour, I am Drake and this is Taime, we have been sent by Kailen."

Bilbo peered cautiously around Ranold at the stranger, and then smiled as he recognized the two men. "Yes, yes come in out of the cold. Ranold start the fire and make some tea to warm our guests."

"No, Master Bilbo, we appreciate your concern but we don't have time. Kailen has asked we bring you back to the fairy compound. We need to be on our way before the snow starts to fall."

Bilbo stepped out onto the porch looking up at the skies, he shivered. The sky was beginning to turn that pinkish color just before it started to snow. He stepped back into the cottage shaking his head in agreement. "From the look of that sky it will snow before morning."

"Make haste, Master Bilbo pack only what you need. We can come back for anything you want after the storm."

"We are already packed," Bilbo smiled as he pointed to the bags by the door.

"Excellent," Drake said. "Now go dress warmly, it's a long ride." He handed the bags to Taime to secure on the horses.

A few minutes later the Bilbo and Ranold emerged from the bedroom dressed, buttoning their heavy coats. "We are ready," Bilbo said, blowing out the candle.

"Let us be off then," Drake said. "Can you ride, Master Bilbo."

No, "I am afraid I cannot..." he stammered looking wide eyed at the mighty Friesian stallion snorting and pawing at the crusted snow.

"Do not be afraid, little Bard, he will not hurt you. I have taken the liberty of making a small bed for you in a carpet bag and Taime has prepared one for Ranold." Drake paused as Bilbo inspected the bag. "You can pull away the flap to watch the progress of our journey or pull it closed to snuggle in the blankets."

"Yes, yes that will do fine," Bilbo said. "Ranold grab a small quilt and pillow for each of us. And grab my cane on your way back." He looked to Drake, "I hope that is alright."

"Yes, of course it is. We want you to be as comfortable as possible." Bilbo watched as Ranold climbed into his carpet bag and was raised then secured to the saddle horn. He climbed into his bag; Drake watched as he buried his cane beneath blankets and wrapped himself in his quilt. He held his breath as he was lifted up and secured to the saddle horn. He felt the saddle shift momentarily as Drake quickly mounted the stallion and felt the great muscles tighten in the horse's shoulder as Drake spurred him into the darkness.

It seemed as though they'd ridden for hours as the horses trudged through the belly deep snow when they heard shouting up ahead. He opened the flap to see what was happening as a dozen riders joined them as they crossed the frozen river heading deep into the land of Fae. The first snowflakes began to fall from the dark, cold sky.

By the time they rode into the village it was snowing heavily, everyone, including the horses, were chilled to the bone. Drake and Taime carefully took their cargo into the great house; they followed a young fairy up the stairs to the guest rooms where Bilbo and Ranold would be sleeping. They placed the carpet bags carefully by the warm fireplace.

"Bilbo, Ranold, we are here," Drake said through chattering teeth. "We will see you at dinner but now we must attend our horses."

Bilbo emerged from the bag cold, weary and sore from being jostled around the carpet bag. He blinked adjusting his eyes to the brightness of the fire. He went to the chair by the fireplace and sat propping his aching leg on the hearth, soaking up the warmth from the flames. Ranold began fussing about the bags folding their blankets.

"Let that go, Ranold. Come sit by the fire and warm up."

"Thank you, Sir," he said as he sat next to Bilbo. "I don't believe I've ever felt so cold in my life."

"I know," he whispered. "But now we are safe, old friend. Now we are safe." He closed his eyes, enjoying the heat.

With a flourish several fairies entered Bilbo's chambers. They brought Bilbo and Ranold's belongings and a tray of snacks and warm wine. "Master Bilbo, I am Dain. I am here to see to your every need." He poured a goblet of wine, handing it to Bilbo and another for Ranold. "Kailen sends his apologies for not being here to greet you but he is attending to some business and will see you at dinner. He wishes for both you and your servant to attend." Dain began unpacking their clothes from their icy bags. He clucked his tongue at each garment he pulled from the bag. Another fairy entered the room, whispered something to Dain in elfin. "Gentleman if you will follow me your bath is ready."

Nearly an hour later Bilbo and Ranold returned to their chambers feeling like themselves again. The fairies had washed, dried and brushed their fur into fluffy delight. The bed had been turned down Bilbo ran his paw along the satin sheet. In the corner a small cot had been placed for Ranold. Bilbo smiled. At the foot of the bed lay two silk tunics, one emerald green for Bilbo and the other a rich brown for Ranold. The attached note said 'wear these for dinner.'

At precisely nine o'clock the dinner bell chimed. Bilbo limped down the hall leaning on Ranold, for support. As they approached the stairs they heard a familiar voice call to them.

"Master Bilbo, I believe this belongs to you." Drake handed Bilbo his cane. "It fell out the bag as we hurried into the lodgings."

Bilbo smiled, taking the cane. "Thank you."

"Would you like some help down those stairs?" Drake did not wait for an answer; he picked up Bilbo with little effort and carried him down the stairs to the great hall. He heard Ranold squeal as Taime picked him up carrying him, as well. As they neared the doors Drake and Taime placed their small friends on the floor so they could walk into the great hall. A hush fell over the room as they entered. Kailen stood to greet the Bard.

"Bilbo, my old friend, come sit beside me. And have some wine." Bilbo walked to the long table calling out greetings to familiar faces of the fairy kingdom, he was pleased to see so many of his old friends. As he came to the tall chair where he was to sit he looked about for way to climb onto it, he was about to ask for help when Drake picked him up and placed him on a stack of pillows piled on the chair. Bilbo laughed, as Drake winked and took the seat beside him. He looked to his left as Taime helped Ranold to his chair.

Bilbo raised his goblet in toast. "To friends…"

"To friends," chimed Kailen. "Bilbo, I am sorry it took so long to get to you. The snows have made it impos4sible to get any wagons through the forest. I was not aware that the situation in the forest was so dire until I got your note. You'll be happy to know your friend the owl is safe and resting in the stable. He was pretty beat up by the winds when he got here. While Drake and Taime came to get you a dozen other men placed bags of food throughout the forest and after this storm stops we will take more food to your forest community."

"Thank you, for your generosity, Lord Kailen. I'm sure there are some very happy tummies in the forest tonight."

"Indeed." Kailen sipped his wine. "Now eat everyone." Bilbo eagerly began to eat. "We have much to discuss after dinner, little Bard."

After the meal was over and the fairy kingdom slowly went to their own quarters Bilbo and Kailen shared another flask of wine as they sat by the fireplace talking quietly. "Bilbo, your leg seems to be paining you more this winter I'll have the physician come up to give you something to ease the pain at bed time."

"It is the cold. It is my own fault with the bitter cold this winter we burnt the wood too fast and when I realizedhow low the wood pile was getting I tried to conserve by heating only one room of the cottage at a time. And now I suffer."

"I have a proposition for you, Bilbo. I know you like to be independent, enjoy living in the forest but this winter has obviously not been good for you. I propose you move here to the fairy realm. You will of course have your own quarters with Ranold. When spring comes and we can get wagons through the forest we will get your belongings and bring them here. You'll be free to come and go as you please but you'll not have the burden of worrying about food and firewood ever again. Not to mention we would enjoy being entertained by your tales on a more regular basis," he paused, taking a drink of wine. "It is a thought, give it some consideration."

Bilbo drank deeply from his wine. He already knew his answer would be yes but didn't want to seem too anxious in his reply. He'd thought many times this winter of asking Kailen if he could move into the Fairy community but didn't know how to gracefully bring up the subject. He would accept the offer in a few days. They sat in silence for a while drinking their wine and enjoying the fire.

“We have house guest we’d like you to meet on the morrow, Bilbo. The birds found a young rabbit wandering in the forest during the storm a couple weeks ago; she was half frozen and delirious by the time we got to her. She was separated from her family as they tried to get to their home on the far side of the forest. I have put word out that she has been found and is recuperating here but no one has come forward. She has responded well to the medicine we have given her but she is despondent I was wondering if you could look in on her perhaps seeing one of her own nd would help her state of mind.”

“Yes, I would be more than happy to talk with her, Kailen. Could I see her tonight?”

“She is sleeping but I see no harm in you looking in on her. Come I’ll show you to her room. The physician has given her a sleeping potion she will not wake.”

They entered her room quietly. She looked so frail and tiny as she lay sleeping. She was white with a black ink spot on her nose and the tip of her left ear. Bilbo thought she looked like an angel as she lay dreaming. His breath caught in his throat he was smitten at first site.

“Do you know her name?” he whispered.

“Yes, it is Lara. Come it is late, let us turn in now. You can meet her after breakfast.”

Bilbo said goodnight to Kailen but remained at the door watching her sleep. He imagined her running through the woods alone and frightened having been separated from her family in the storm. He thought back to a time when he was snared in a hunter’s trap, how his family had tried to free him but couldn’t and his father’s painful decision to leave him behind to die in the trap. He would never forget his mother’s tears as she said goodbye to him. Tears ran down his furry cheeks as he remembered that day. But like Lara, he had been found by the Fairies and was nursed back to health. He turned to go to his room and heard her cry out in her sleep, his heart ached as he listened to her nurse console her from the frightening dream.

Ranold had gone to bed after dinner and was in a deep slumber in his new bed. Bilbo quickly undressed and put on the fresh night shirt Dain had left for him and as he settled back into bed he thought of the frail rabbit down the hall. "Lara," he whispered into the darkness.

Bilbo rose late in the morning, feeling rested for the first time in weeks. Ranold brought him some tea and cereal for breakfast. He dismissed Ranold for the day, telling him to explore the village. He dressed quickly in the vest and suit coat left hanging by the bed and hurried down the hall to meet Lara. She was sitting up in bed wearing a pretty pink bed jacket as he peered into the room.

He cleared his throat and knocked on the door. "May I come in?"

She looked up expecting to see one of the Fairies come to check on her, to her surprise it was Bilbo. Her eyes lit up at the site of another rabbit. "Oh yes, please do," she said in a shy voice.

"Lord Kailen told me what happened to you and I wanted to meet you. I am Bilbo," he said as he bowed.

"I know who you are…you are the Bard from the Yule celebration. I am Lara."

"You were at the festival?" he said trying to remember if he had seen her face in the crowd.

"I am sorry to hear you got lost in the storm, but I know the Fairies have taken good care of you."

"Yes, they have but I miss my family so much."

"Kailen has put the word out that you are safe and hopefully your family will come for you in the spring."

"I know you are trying to cheer me up Bilbo but they will not, I know my father and he will not come." she looked away.

"Lara, perhaps when you are feeling better you'd like to walk around the village with me."

"I'd like that…" she said in a tiny voice. She smiled sweetly at him.

"Good, then I will check in on you later and see how you are feeling." Bilbo smiled his heart racing.

Over the next few weeks Bilbo rose early and went to visit Lara. He read to her, recited tales of the Fae as well as the forest creatures and had a small harp brought in her room so he could play and sing for her. He took most of his meals with her making sure she ate all her food so she would regain her strength faster. One morning he was in the kitchen overseeing her morning tray when felt a tiny paw on his shoulder.

"If it's alright Bilbo I'd like to take my meal here in the kitchen with you," Lara said.

Bilbo laughed. "It is so good to see you up…have a seat my dear one."

"Perhaps we can go for that walk today, if you've nothing else to do," Lara looked up at him batting her eyelashes. Bilbo nearly dropped his tea cup as he realized she was flirting with him. That afternoon they went walking and from that day forward they were steady companions.

On Imbolg Lara and Bilbo went for their daily walk, an uplifting tune of springtime was on the wind, they laughed as they walked joking that the badger had seen his shadow and there would be several more weeks of snow. Lara looked down at her feet and saw a tiny purple crocus peeking through the snow. Bilbo smiled; he took it as an omen for the future, for new life and a life with Lara. He walked her to room and kissed her on the cheek. Lara blushed and held her paw to her cheek as he limped away. She had fallen in love with Bilbo.

Later that evening Bilbo knocked on Kailen's door. "Bilbo, come in. Sit and have a drink with me." Bilbo took the goblet of wine and began to pace the room. "What troubles you, my friend?" Kailen asked, genuinely concerned.

"Kailen, I have decided to take you up on your offer and live here," he said as he sat down.

"That is excellent news, though I must say I was beginning to think you were going to say no, it has been several weeks since I made the offer."

"No, I have just been preoccupied."

"That is an understatement if ever I heard one, Bilbo," Kailen laughed. "She is a lovely preoccupation, I might add." Bilbo blushed.

"Kailen, I am in love with Lara. From that first moment I saw her I knew she was the one. I am going to ask her to be my wife. If she will have me…"

"If she will have you…. Oh, Bilbo have you not seen the way she looks at you. She talks of you constantly. When are you going to ask her?"

"I thought on the morrow when we are out for our walk."

"Why wait? Ask her tonight. There is magic a foot on this night."

Bilbo thought for a moment. "You are right. I have waited my whole life for this lovely creature and this is amagical night." He drank the rest of his wine and went in search of Lara.

He found her in the great hall sitting in front of the fireplace in a long lavender dress listening intently to one of Drake's great adventures. She was even lovelier in the firelight if that was possible. She smiled when she saw Bilbo walking towards her.

"Forgive me for interrupting your story Drake but I need a word with Lara." He held her paw and looked deeply into her eyes.

"We'll give you some privacy, Master Bilbo," Drake said, but before the Fairies could turn away Bilbo painfully got down on one knee.

"Lara, I love you with all my heart. Will you marry me?"

"Oh yes, of course I will," she said with tears of joy streaming down her tiny, furry cheeks. "Bilbo, I've dreamed of you asking me to be your wife." She helped Bilbo get back up, they embraced, and shared their first kiss. Drake and the other fairies clapped and congratulated the couple. Kailen watched from the doorway nodding his approval.

They celebrated into the wee hours of the morn, drinking wine and sharing kisses. At last Bilbo walked Lara to her room and kissed her long and sweetly. He bid her goodnight after several more kisses and went to his room. As he undressed and got into his night shirt he knew he had never been happier in his life. He crawled under the thick layers of covers, resting his head back onto the pillow, grinning from ear to ear. He and Lara would soon be wed, and with a little luck there would be babies by late spring. He pulled the covers close and looked out the window into the starry, starry night.

Twilight's Song

The days are growing dim and cold
I find myself in the twilight of my years
Longing for the youth
Wasted away on trivialities
Squandered in drunken disarray
And material frivolities
The high-flying pilot of erotic desires
Bound to the self-possessing pleasures
With no regard to anything
But the satisfaction of inner sanction
As the night falls I find myself
Longing to surrender
To the days of my pride.

SERENITY

Night creeping shadow cast
One man upon the glory
Of a royal court
Serene in the sky
Voices eco, uniting
Sound blaring
Shattering Mother earth's
Supreme silence
Like a king he wails pawns watch in awe Signs of change in the air
Perpetually wandering

Lady Day

Lady, you wake with the sun
Golden ray's stream
Through your hair
Full of warmth
You look so eloquent
In all your finery

Nights you spend contemplating
Dreaming shades of past
Not beholding thoughts of
Mere mortal man
Immortality shall be yours

Bounding through fields
Flowing with brightness
Gently caressing my mind
You're so free
So full of life

Late at night I watch you sleeping
Sugar plums dancing
A slight smile kissed
With gentle rays

The Mourning Dew

Time and space weaved and intertwined, light blended into dark, the seasons came and went, the years rolled by like the billowy clouds in the sky in the land of the Fae. The days grew warmer, the cold winds of winter had given way to the spring thaw and the snows had turned to rain. Everyone scampered about making ready for the spring Equinox celebration. Lara tried to get in the spirit by baking some of her sweet, treats but her heart just wasn't in the festive spirit this spring. She pulled the last of the treats from the oven and placed them on a rack to cool. She pulled off her apron and called to Ranold she was going for a walk.

The sun felt good on her back as she strolled through the garden just beyond the great house. The first of the spring flowers had bloomed overnight painting a sea of pastel as far as the eye could see. Lara drank in the fragrance with each deep breath, chided herself for not coming to the garden since the snows had melted. She paused at the bottom of the knoll before climbing up the gentle slope to tiny grave at the top. Her breath caught in her chest as she reached the top of the hill and tears began to run down her cheeks. The Fairies had erected a beautiful marble grave stone the color of the rose-tinted morning sky. Lara placed a tiny bouquet at the base of the marker and lovingly traced the carefully etched words on the stone. "Bilbo the Bard...Lord of the Forest."

She sat down beside the grave, sobbing heavily. It had been nearly seven months since Bilbo had died peacefully during his afternoon nap. Lara had found him when she went to wake him for dinner. The Fairy physician had said his heart had just given out. She cried until there were no more tears to cry and watched as the Fairies had sealed Bilbo in his velvet bed to sleep for eternity. The world had stopped when they placed the tiny casket in the cold, black earth. The land of Fae and the creatures of the forest had come far and wide to pay their respects to the little Bard. Lara was deeply moved at the sympathetic out pouring it helped ease the pain but her heart ached and had taken to her bed shortly after the wake to mourn her beloved. Kailen worried over her as she had grown thin and despondent, ordered a nurse to watch over both her and Ranold day and night. It felt as though a dark cloud had been placed over the forest.

At Samhain Lara made her first appearance since Bilbo's passing. She hadn't felt like making a public appearance but went to show support of Bilbo's apprentice, a young silver fox from France named Aramis. Aramishad been so nervous, afraid he'd not be able to fulfill his new role as Bard of the Forest. Lara had taken her place at the Fairy's table that night to honor the dead, dressed in her finest black dress. After the dinner she listened to the stories the ancestors, she cried as Aramis had sung a song in tribute to Bilbo and laughed at his feeble attempts of humor and listened in awe as he recited some the stories Bilbo had so eloquently composed. At Yule she'd gone through the motions of the holidays, her heart aching silently. Ranold did his best to help her get through it.

She had remained reclusive throughout the winter but with spring in the air she was starting to feel herself again. She looked out over the garden and smiled sadly. Bilbo would have appreciated the view of garden. Kailen had been right in suggesting she bury her husband here. She sighed wishing Bilbo could see his favorite time of year.

"My Bilbo, I miss you so," she whispered to the wind.

The sun had begun to set low on the western horizon; she pulled her shawl tightly about her shoulders as she began the descent down the slope. She'd been gone far longer than she'd planned; she knew Ranold would be beside himself with worry. As she hurried along the darkening path she caught her hem on rock, tripping and landing heavily on her paw trying to break the fall. She cried out in pain.

"Madame Lara, are you alright?" Aramis called as he rushed to her from another path that wound through the garden.

"Yes, of course I am," she said through clinched teeth, trying not to cry.

"Let me help you Madame," Aramis said reaching for her injured paw to pull her up. She winched with pain and began to cry. "Oh Madame, I am so sorry, I have hurt you and I was only trying to help..."

"No, Aramis, it was not your fault I hurt it when I fell," she said wiping away the tears.

"We must get you to the physician immediately," Aramis fussed.

"Just walk me home. Ranold will be so worried that I'm out so late."

"Ranold can wait, Madame..."

"Aramis please, just see me home and I'll have Ranold send for the physician." She straightened her dress and pulled her shawl tight around her slender form. "Let me have my dignity I feel so stupid having fallen in the first place."

Aramis smiled. "As you wish Madame I will get you home safely." He bowed and offered her his arm. Lara laughed, in spite of her aching paw took hold of his arm.

"What are you doing in the garden this late in the evening?"

"Madame, I was on my way to talk with Monsieur Bilbo when I saw you sitting on the hill, and I did not want to disturb you."

"You talk with him too?" she said.

"Oh yes, I always sought his council when he was alive why should it be different now? He hears me from wherever he is now and sends me a sign."

"And I thought I was just being a foolish, old woman wasting away my days talking to his grave..."

“You are not foolish or old Madame. Anyone who thinks so has not experienced the love you and Monsieur Bilbo had.”

Lara smiled sadly as they walked up the steps to her door. “Thank you, Aramis. You have been a good friend to me during this trying time…” she stopped, her voice breaking.

“Jet`aime mon amie,” Aramis put his paw around her trembling shoulders. “I miss him too.”

Ranold slammed the door shut loudly behind him as he headed down the stairs with Lara’s coat. “Lara,’ I have been so worried,” he said placing the coat around her shoulders.

“I am alright Ranold.” She smiled warmly and winked at Aramis.

“Then perhaps I will see you at dinner, Madame.” He bowed and turned to go. “Do not forget to get your paw looked at.” He began to hum as he walked away.

Lara listened for a moment to the unfamiliar tune. “Aramis,” she called. “What is that tune you hum?”

“Something I have composed for the spring equinox. You will hear it in its entirety on the morrow.” He turned to walk away once again.

“Aramis wait…” she called after him. “Would you have dinner with me? I do not wish to dine alone tonight.”

“Yes, Madame Lara, I would be honored,” he said. “I will come by for you at a quarter past nine so we make a grand entrance into the great hall. Now I must go I have an important meeting with someone.” He winked and bowed low.

Lara watched him fade into the evening shadows. She shivered and pulled her coat tight as she looked up into the darkening sky; the first stars were beginning to twinkle on the horizon. In the kitchen Ranold was brewing a pot of tea, the aroma of her sweet treats still lingering in the air. She tossed her coat across a chair and sat down, her paw was beginning to throb.

“Ranold I need you to send for the physician and then…”

“Lara are you ill?” Ranold said as he ran to her side.

"I fell and I've hurt my paw," she said, "Now please stop your fussing and send for the physician. And bring me a cup of tea while I wait."

Lara sat in front of the fireplace in the sitting room waiting for Aramis. She absently fingered the tiny crystals sewn on the sleeves of her black velvet gown. The physician had bandaged her paw to keep it from swelling and had given her a small potion for the pain. She wanted nothing more than to crawl into bed and dream of days past but she knew she was expected to make an appearance in the great hall.

"Ranold, hurry up. Aramis will be here soon," she said. "You take longer than a young princess trying on every gown she owns to get ready."

"I am ready," Ranold said sarcastically. "I do not see why I must join the two of you for dinner."

"Because I want you there and we go to show our support of Aramis."

"As you wish, Madame," Ranold bowed exaggeratedly then took the seat beside her. Lara laughed.

"Why do you dislike Aramis so?"

"Why are you so taken with that rogue, Lara? He dresses like a dandy; he doesn't show the reverence to his position that Bilbo did and that accent of his, it is so thick you could cut it with a knife. It is said he has a kit in every hamlet..." Ranold said.

Lara waved her paw. "Enough of this foolish talk Ranold obviously Bilbo saw something in him you do not. He dresses in his own style if he did not, he'd simply be trying to copy Bilbo. That lovely French accent just adds to his charm. As for the rumors about having a kit in every hamlet I sincerely doubt it but what if he does? What he does on his own time is his business. Bilbo once told me those very rumors went around about him."

"Lara in the months he has been Bard he has done nothing but steal Bilbo's speeches and songs he has not composed anything new..." Ranold protested.

"That is not true Ranold and you know it," she looked sternly at her old friend. "Yes, he has been reciting Bilbo's compositions and singing his songs, that is what a bard does. The legends are passed down from generation to generation and added upon with each new Bard. Aramis has been reciting Bilbo's stories as a tribute to him; he is not stealing my husband's work. Every night he sings songs passed down through the generations in the great hall along with new ones he is writing daily. With the Spring Equinox celebration he will begin telling tales he has written. You judge him far too harshly."

"I did not mean to upset you, Lara," he said looking away to the fire.

"Well, you have. I cannot believe you listen to the gossip of those who were jealous of Bilbo's decision to mentor a fox. I will hear no more of this talk. Try to be pleasant when Aramis gets here." They sat in silence watching the fire dance upon the logs in the fireplace.

At a quarter past nine Aramis arrived to accompany Lara to dinner. Ranold reluctantly tagged along behind them as they walked through winding hallways to the great hall. When they entered the room a hush fell over the crowd as they watched Aramis walk regally in his red velvet frock coat to the main table with Lara on his arm. Lara could feel the eyes upon them, hear the whispers as she greeted Kailen and his wife, she smiled warmly to all as Aramis helped her onto her chair. Lara settled back to enjoy her meal; she had not realized how famished she was. She watched with amusement as the gossips speculated about their grand entrance.

As the meal wound down and the food trenchers were cleared from the tables Aramis took his place in the center of the room where he sang several songs passed down from the ancients, he sang a love ballad that Bilbo had written for Lara and then moved from the harp to play his mandolin and sang several songs he had written. The crowd grew silent as he adeptly played an instrumental on his mandolin, cheering for more when he stood and bowed signifying the end of the evening's entertainment.

Lara smiled as he returned to the great table and handed him a goblet of wine. "You begin to win them over, Aramis," she whispered. Aramis smiled warmly and drank from his wine.

"I hope so Madame," he said. "I hope so."

Lara and Aramis joined Kailen and a small group gathering around the fireplace, the conversation was lively, the wine flowed freely, and Lara realized she was actually enjoying herself. The healing process was beginning, she was still sad but she had missed the companionship of her friends, Bilbo would always be with her, it was time to start enjoying the gift of life once again.

One by one dinner revelers drifted out of the great hall and on to their bed chambers. Lara and Aramis sat talking and sipping wine until the wee hours of the morning. Conversation came so easily as if they had been friends in several life times. She saw more and more what Bilbo had seen in him and why he had taken such pains to teach him everything he knew about being a bard. As Aramis went to get them another goblet of wine she remembered the day the Fairies had brought the small, bedraggled fox to the physician to heal. He was about a year old and been left for dead with a hunter's arrow through his shoulder. They were not sure he would pull through after having lain in the pouring rain and having gone without food for so long. It was slow but he'd made a full recovery and Bilbo had taken an immediate liking to him and began mentoring him a short time later. She knew Bilbo would have been so proud of the way he had conducted himself tonight.

Lara yawned as Aramis handed her the wine. "Madame, you grow weary, and the hour grows late, we should call it a night after we finish this drink," he said laughing.

"Yes, I suppose we should. I have enjoyed this evening. Thank you for being my friend, Aramis," she said as she yawned again.

"The pleasure is mine, Madame Lara," he raised his goblet in toast. "What should we drink to?"

Lara thought for a moment then smiled and raised her goblet, "To the Fairy blood in us." Aramis smiled nodding in agreement and drank deeply of the wine.

Lara rose from her slumber around three in the afternoon. Ranold had left her a note that he'd gone to help set up for the festivities. She brewed a cup of tea and went out onto the porch to enjoy the beauty of the lovely spring day. It felt good just to sit under the sun's warm rays. She knew she couldn't sit around long though as she had much to do before evening fell. Reluctantly she went inside to her room. Lara threw open the doors to her closet trying to decide what to wear. She was in the mood to wear something bright, colorful but it was too soon to shed her widow's weeds. Finally, she decided on a satin gown with black pearl buttons and the multicolored shawl Bilbo had given her last spring. As she laid the gown out on the bed she thought of her conversation with Ranold the night before. She told herself not to be so hard on him. He had been with her husband far longer than she had and his world had been turned inside out when Bilbo died. He'd been Bilbo's manservant since he was young and he was lost without someone to dote over. She turned to close the closet door but stopped when she saw Bilbo's royal blue velvet suit coat, Ranold had always admired it, she would give it to him to show how much she valued his friendship. She left it on his bed with a note that said simply "for you my old friend."

Lara dressed quickly and went to the garden to pick a bouquet of fresh flowers for Bilbo. She wanted to say happy spring to him before the night's revelry began. When she got to the top of the knoll she stopped, her heart skipped a beat as she watched Aramis loving unfolding a blanket of flowers on Bilbo's grave. The fairies had placed hundreds of candles around the shrine to be lit at dusk to honor the little Bard. Tears flowed freely down her cheeks. She smiled sadly at Aramis but couldn't find the words to say what she was feeling. Aramis simply smiled back and wrapped his paw lovingly around her shoulder. They stood in silence for a few moments then headed back to the garden. The bells began to toll from the tower high above the great house signaling spring arrived. Aramis walked Lara to her to seat in front of the stage. He bowed and went to get ready for his presentation after the fairies performed the spring equinox ritual. Lara called excitedly to her children gathering nearby.

The crowd grew silent as Kailen and several other fairies took the stage to bless the return of the spring and the birth of all the wonders of nature and all the new babies being born to the creatures of the forest ensuring the cycle of life continue for generations to come. They blessed the seeds to be planted in the coming weeks so there would be a bountiful harvest and said, a prayer of hope, peace and happiness for their forest realm. They ended the ritual with a chant from the ancient elfin language and silently left the stage.

Moments later Aramis strutted on the stage in a plum-colored brocade frock coat, a black tri-cornered hat with purple and green plumes and thigh high boots. He sat his mandolin down carefully at the edge of the stage. He waited as Bilbo had taught him for the crowd to hush.

"My friends of the forest we are gathered here tonight to celebrate the arrival of spring. We bless the seeds we are to plant so they may bring us luscious bounty at the fall harvests. We are here to marvel at the re-birth of the land, the warming sun and precious life that grows in the bellies of many of our forest friends. We gather to feast, share a few cups of wine and talk with old friends." He paused making sure all were listening. "And we gather to pay homage to Bilbo, Lord of the Forest," he pointed to the hill where the candles had been lit, illuminating the final resting place of their beloved little Bard. "Let us no longer be sad at his passing and remember what joy he brought us in his time as the balladeer. This was his favorite time year when the flowers begin bloom after a long winter's night, when the sun begins to shine warmly on our backs and babies are born. It was also, the time when Monsieur Bilbo and Madame Lara pledged their vows of undying love to each other. Over the years they had many children who in turn produced many grandchildren and great grandchildren. Monsieur Bilbo has left us with a rich legacy, a tall order to fill and as the reigning Bard of the Forest I will do my best to carry on that legacy but from this night forward I will begin to make this position of high esteem my own." He looked around the crowd and then at Lara and winked as she nodded her approval.

"I now have a surprise for you Madame Lara. Your great granddaughter, Pearlie has given birth to her babes." Pearlie shyly walked on to the stage carrying a basket of seven babies. "Pearlie has named her first born son in honor of her great grandfather," Aramis reached into the basket and carefully pulled a small white rabbit from its bed. He held him high for all to see. "I give you Bilbo." The creatures of the forest cheered as Aramis walked about the stage holding the baby. He stopped in the middle of the stage and looked to the hill holding the baby high into the air and said, "Is he not cute, Monsieur Bilbo?"

Aramis cradled the baby tightly as he walked from the stage to Lara. "Madame here is your first great-great grandson." He placed the babe in Lara's arms; tears of joy ran down her cheeks.

"Look he has your ink spot on his nose…I will give him the nickname Ink Spot." Lara laughed as she hugged the baby and motioned for Pearlie to bring the rest of the babies and join her.

Aramis returned to the stage and began playing his mandolin until the revelers settled down. After several minutes passed a hush fell over the crowd as they realized he was going to grace them with a ballad. He hummed a few bars and then began to sing in his deep, rich voice.

"The moon and stars
Twinkle in the velvet
Sea of darkness
Giving way to the
Bright days of sunshine
As we break the from winter's bond
Awakening to the dawn of spring

And the warm days ahead
The heavens grace us
With the gentle nurturing rains
The world comes alive
As we dance through the hills and
Valleys in the morning dew
May gladness spring forth
On this joyous Eostre
Blessed be, blessed be.

Phantom

I rise with the twilight
Like a vampire from the tomb
And roam the streets of darkness
Drowning out sorrows
I suck the night dry of emotion
Stumbling home before the light of day
To sink beneath the silken sheets
And summon memories
Of faded yesterdays

DARK ABYSS

Light unto my darkness
Shed thy everlasting
Glow unto the abyss
Of my barren soul
Lying dormant along the
Oceans of an unsung melody

Drown out the multitude
Of voices pounding out the
Monotonous notes that
Nightly creeps through my brain
Ripping the madness
Along my body
As the everlasting tune
Marches on never to be heard

But for eternity
To haunt my dreams

Visions

Cold abandoned room
A cavern deep within
My mind where silent screams
Echo along the galaxy
Of forgotten memories
That dance upon
The seas of time
Dangling in quiet repose
Darkness, darkness
Wrapped in the embrace of
Your loving arms

Witch Hallow

"Nadine," the whisper flowed on the night breeze. "Nadine, come to us."

Nadine woke with a start from a dream filled with dancing and laughter and giant bonfires illuminating the hills just beyond the meadow. She heard someone calling her name, felt a hand reaching out to her pulling her into the dark night. She sat up in bed trying to shake the dream. The light of the full moon peaked through the burlap curtain covering her window. She felt a cold nose nudge her hand from beside the bed; she patted the bedcovers inviting her faithful hound, Blu onto the bed. She hugged him tight as she listened to the voices call from the darkness.

She wanted to go back to sleep, she had a long day ahead of her with all the chores but she knew sleep was lost with the voices calling to her. She rubbed her brow thinking she must be going mad. The voices had started about a month ago when she went to the meadow to gather a bouquet of the first wildflowers of the season. Her name floated distinctly on the gentle breeze that had come out of nowhere from the hills just to the west of the meadow. She dropped the flowers in surprise and looked around but no one was there. Even Blu had looked to the west in search of the voices. She had gathered up her flowers thinking it was her brothers playing a joke on her. She could picture them hiding amongst the bushes snickering, she'd not give them the satisfaction of letting them know they had scared her and went about gathering more flowers. She called to Blu and headed towards the path leading home.

Three nights later she heard the voices again calling her name as she carried the bucket of dirty dishwater out onto the back stoop after dinner. The handle had slipped out her hand, the water spilling over the porch as the bucket landed on the rotting planks. Her breath caught in the back of her throat as she listened to her name on the wind. "Nadine."

"What the hell you doing out there girl?" her father called out.

"I tripped, Pa..." she stuttered. "I dropped the bucket of dishwater is all."

"Well, see you clean up your mess and fetch me another jug."

"Yes, Pa," she said absently peering into darkening horizon. She saw Blu in the distance heading towards the sounds of the voices and called him back to the house.

That night she had tossed and turned dreaming of a herd of deer running in the woods and a faceless young man running effortlessly after them with a bow and arrow in his hand. He was lean and tall; his skin was tanned golden brown, polished with oils, gleaming in the sunlight as his muscles rippled with each stride as he chased the deer, his huntsman running close behind. She awoke as he let loose his arrow to bring down the stag.

The dreams always came three nights in a row and then nothing for days, but the voices called to her nightly in her sleep, as she worked around the cabin and especially when she neared the edge of the meadow closest to the woods where the land gently sloped into the hills. She'd been forbidden to go there since she was a child, when her Ma had run away.

Nadine climbed quietly out of bed, wrapping a blanket around her night gown and tip toed towards the parlor. The cabin was quiet and dark, except for the faint light of the dying embers in the fireplace at the far side of the room. Her father sat sleeping in the old easy chair by the hearth, a shotgun lying across his lap, the jug of whisky lay at his feet. The old clock on the mantel began to chime the hour; one, two then three o'clock...the witching hour. She stopped as the voices grew louder and swirled about the room she could feel invisible hands grabbing for her pushing her towards the door, feel their breath upon her skin as she stifled a scream forming in her throat. She felt dizzy, felt the room spinning beneath her feet.

"Where you think you're going, girl?" her father bellowed.

Nadine jumped, trying to steady her racing heart, thankful the voices had stopped. "Why you always gotta be scaring me like that, Pa?" she said.

"Cause you're always sneakin' around in the dark…just like your worthless whore of a Ma did. I ain't putting up with that with you, Nadine."

"I was not sneakin', around and you're drunk," she said trying to calm her racing heart.

"I ain't near drunk enough," he muttered, reaching for the jug at his feet. "I asked where you was going."

"Outside to sit to in the rocking chair for a bit, I can't sleep," she said.

"Dressed like that? Only whores go out into dark dressed in their night clothes."

"I got a blanket wrapped around me, Pa. Ain't nobody gonna see me sitting on the porch this time of night," she said pulling the blanket tighter.

"More likely you was going to meet some boy."

"I ain't got no beau," she said. "You know that you scare away any suitors that might come calling."

"Suitors," he laughed. "More like young bucks sniffin' for a roll in the hay. They all heard tell of your Ma and figure you're just like her."

"I ain't Ma stop saying that," she turned to go back to bed, tears starting to run down her cheeks.

"Think I don't hear that boy calling your name late at night?" he called after her. I'm telling ya now I ain't gonna put up with some bastard coming around here gettin' you with child. Don't think I haven't noticed how you fill out them clothes you wear. You look mighty fetchin' in your Ma's old dresses you been wearin'. Think it's high time to find you a husband whilst you are still a maiden. I don't want some bastard's whelp runnin' around here after that celebration in the hills. I ain't gonna be disgraced a second time."

"I don't want no husband and there ain't gonna be no bastards running around," she said through the tears

"You hush and get back to bed. Your Gran ain't around to stop me from marryin' you off anymore." He took another swig from the jug. "If I had my way you'd been married and have children by now. Shoot, you're nearly sixteen, well past your prime as it is."

"I don't want no husband," she protested.

"Hush. Get on back to bed before I take a mind to whip you," he snickered as he reached for the jug.

Nadine bit off the words forming on her tongue and went back to her room. She crawled into bed pulling the covers tight, Blu climbed onto the bed with her as she pulled him close. Her father heard the voices too, she smiled into the darkness; she wasn't going crazy after all. She fell back to sleep, dreaming of the bonfires that filled the hillside on Walpurgis Night.

The sun was peaking over the trees on the eastern horizon when she woke. She dressed hurriedly and went to the kitchen to start a fire in the cook stove. She peered into the parlor where he father still slept then grabbed her basket to gather eggs from the hen coup. Blu ran ahead barking, searching for a rabbit or bird to chase. She looked about the yard, she loved this time of morning when the sun was just starting to grow in the sky, the air was still cool and the dew starting to roll off the grass. She saw one of her brothers come out of the barn and stretch in the morning sun; he yawned and called to another brother on the stoop to wake up.

"You boys drink too much hooch last night? Nadine laughed as she called to her brother. "Couldn't ya make it into bed?"

"Funny, Nadine," her brother called back as he walked towards her. "I wish that were it. Pa's been making us stay up at night watching for that boy he hears calling your name late at night. You got a beau you're sneakin' around with, girl?"

"No, I ain't, Carl," she said. "Pa was yellin' at me about hearin' voices last night..."

"We heard. What was ya doing up so late, girl?" Carl said. "You ever hear voices, Nadine? Tell me true, girl

"No, I ain't," she said praying he wouldn't see the lie in her eyes. "You ever hear this boy calling me in the night, Carl?"

"Pa swears he hears him," Carl said looking away. "He says them voices are getting stronger every night. Pa's been drinkin' hard since the voices started. He always does this time of year."

"Think he misses Ma?" Nadine whispered.

"In his own way, mostly I think it just galls him the way she left us," Carl looked down at his little sister and hugged her tight. "He's afraid the witch blood runs in your veins, too. You best get breakfast ready before he wakes up."

Nadine went back to the cabin and began cooking breakfast. The aroma of the thick slices of fat back pork, potatoes and eggs soon drifted through the cabin and out into the morning air. Blu came running home sniffing the air, hoping for a scrap or two to be thrown his way. Nadine filled her brother's plates and was filling her own when her father staggered into the room.

"Smells good, girl. I gotta say one thing for your Gran she sure did teach you how to cook." Nadine hurried to set the plate for her Pa. She dished up another for herself and took her seat in the corner by the door. "I'm sure gonna miss your cooking, Nadine. But I'm gonna find you a husband and get you promised before this heathen nonsense up in them hills."

"But Pa..."

"No, girl there's no discussin' this. My mind's made up. Joe Crawford's made a mighty tempting offer for your hand and I'm gonna talk with him this afternoon," he said as he shoved another bit of eggs and potatoes in his mouth. "Now get done with your meal you've got a lot of chores to do today. If you get done early, you can go do whatever you want."

Nadine didn't feel much like eating after that and toyed with her food until everyone was done eating. After breakfast she cleared the table and washed the dishes. She went out into the yard to gather the freshly killed chickens her brothers had left for her to clean for dinner. As she plucked the feathers from the birds she began to think about her Gran and how she'd taught her to grab each feather one by one and pull it back and away from the bird. She missed Gran, she'd had raised her after Ma ran off, taught her everything she knew. Gran had even taught her the old ways in secret so they wouldn't be lost to the future. Nadine knew what herbs to pick for cooking, which ones for healing and what signs to look for in nature when seasons were about to change. But most importantly Gran had taught her the magic of her people who lived deep in the hills, who had brought those beliefs from across the sea, handing them down from generation to generation.

Late in the afternoon Nadine put the freshly baked loaves of bread by the widow to cool and cut up the vegetables she gathered from the root cellar to add to the chickens roasting in the pot on the old cook stove. She took off her apron, threw it on the chair and called to Blu as she ran out the door and headed towards the creek. She felt like a slave in this household of men and now her father wanted to make her a slave to another man. She wanted to run away.

She ran like the wind to the creek, Blu running by her side, barking all the way. She lay back against the old willow tree trying to catch her breath. She wasn't going to let her father marry her off to that stinky old Joe Crawford. She'd run far away before she'd let him touch her. She looked into the sky and closed her eyes as Gran's lovely old face drifted across her mind. Gran had died last summer and there wasn't a day she didn't think of her.

She thought back to the night Gran had died. She'd been ill for some months and finally taken to her bed. Nadine had always held out hope Gran would get better but when she heard her father talk of taking Gran's body into the hills to her people to be honored, she knew the end was near. The night she had died Nadine had been called to her bedside to say goodbye. There had been urgency in the old woman's final words to her.

"Nadine, when the time comes when the voices call to you go to them and do not look back. Do not be afraid, they mean you no harm. They wish you to claim your rightful place. Run like the wind to them, child. Never look back it is your destiny."

Gran had died in her arms moments later. Pa had a small service for her in the meadow before he and her brothers headed up the winding road into the hills taking Gran to her people. She had not been allowed to go, staying behind with her oldest brother. She'd watched through her tears as the tiny wagon disappeared into the hills. Later the night she had watched a single bonfire light up the hills, she knew it wasn't a fire of the festivals but her Gran's funeral pyre. She had watched from the back stoop until the wee hours of the morning when her brother finally carried her to bed.

As the sun began to grow low in the western sky Nadine reluctantly called to Blu and headed back to the cabin. She picked a bouquet of flowers along the way to put on the dinner table. Gran's words kept running through her mind. She'd had known the voices would come. Nadine searched her memories for the stories of the old ways and what the voices meant. After dinner Nadine went to bed early. She fell asleep with Blu stretched out beside her.

The voices called insistently on the night wind. "Nadine! Come Nadine!"

As the weeks passed the dreams became more vivid and voices became louder as they called to her. Blu perked his ears every time he heard the voices staying close by her side. She woke early one morning to the sound of something hitting against her window after a dream about a blonde-haired man with finely chiseled features running through the woods. When she opened the curtain a garland of greenery and wildflowers hung from her window frame. She threw back the burlap curtain and reached out the window to pull it down before anyone saw. Three days later a second garland was hung gently tapping the window frame in the morning breeze. She hurriedly pulled it down and stuffed it under her bed with the other one.

Nadine sat on the stoop watching many of her neighbors cut through the woods that bordered the hills on their way to Beltane on the morrow. After dinner her father began drinking heavily, sending her to bed early. As she lay in the darkness she heard the key turn, locking her in her room. "You can come out when this fool celebration is over, hear me girl." He slammed his fist into the wall and stumbled to his chair in the parlor.

She called to Blu and pulled him close as he climbed onto the bed. She sobbed into his soft fur until she fell into a deep slumber. She dreamed of being bathed by women, her skin rubbed and polished with oils until it shinned in the candlelight. She was led to a small cave carved into the hillside. There her attendants drew ancient markings on her skin and guided her to a bed. She was instructed to lie on a bed made of animal furs and was covered in blankets made of red and gold silk. Candles were lit, their flames casting shadows on the walls of the cave. The man from hunt stood in the cave entrance looking at her. He dropped his bow and crossed the room to her side. He leaned down and kissed her lips and pulled the silk blankets away from her naked body and pulled his loin cloth off as he lay down beside her on the bed…

Nadine awoke just before dawn to Blu barking. She patted his head and pulled the curtain away from the window to see what he was so excited about. A garland made of greenery and white wildflowers hung around her window gently blowing in the morning breeze. She heard shouting outside her window and fell back onto her bed. Her door burst open moments later, her father angrily throwing the garland at her. She cowered in her bed as he shouted and threatened to beat her. At last, he slammed the door shut and stomped into the parlor yelling at her brothers.

"I told you she had a boy she was sneakin' around with," he shouted. "But everyone thinks I'm just drinking too much. Well, what the hell is that garland about then? You all know what that means." He sat down in the chair by the fire and reached for his jug.

"You better hope Joe don't get wind of this, or he won't marry her. By God I'll beat some answers outta her." He headed back to the bedroom.

Carl stepped in front of him blocking his way. "You ain't gonna beat her old man and there ain't gonna be a wedding…

"You talk big son," Pa bellowed. "Get out of my way."

Carl didn't budge, held his ground steady. "Joe already knows about the garlands Pa," Carl said. "I told him when she found the second yesterday. He don't want no part of a witch's daughter."

"Why I ought to beat you boy." Pa raised his hand to strike Carl.

"Don't even think about hitting me old man, I ain't a little boy no more," Carl shouted. "You know as well as I do where that garland came from. It's the same with the voices, she belongs to them and they want her where she belongs…Pa, she aint' got no lover. I follow her when she goes on her walks up the road, the meadow and the creek, she don't talk to no one…that dog is the only one ever around her."

"You hear the voices? he said taking a step back from his son.

"Course I do…same as I heard them five years ago when they called for me." Carl watched his father's eyes grew wide with fear. "I went when it was my turn to run with the stag and I sired me beautiful baby girl who lives in them hills with her ma waitin' for me. I only came back here cause I promised Gran I'd watch over Nadine."

"You blasphemous traitor," Pa shouted. "Get out of my house."

"With pleasure old man I don't belong here anymore than she does, but I will not leave without Nadine." Carl watched the old man go back into the parlor and slump into his chair. "Nadine, come here."

Nadine walked into the parlor, Blu by her side growling lowly, protectively. She looked at her brothers and to her father.

"Nadine, I'm leavin' to live in the hills are you comin' with me?" Carl said.

She looked at her brother and smiled. "Me and Blu is coming with you Carl. I want to see my Ma and I want to take my place at Beltane. She looked at her father a few moments, "I do love you but the need to take my place among my people is greater than..." she left the rest unsaid.

"You ain't taking her nowhere, boy. Get out of my house."

"Time you knew the truth, girl…" Carl said.

"Shut your mouth boy," Pa yelled.

"No, you shut yours, old man. I'm tired of keeping your secrets," Carl growled. "Ma didn't runaway, Nadine. The night she was gonna take you, me and Gran to our kin Pa shot her dead and buried her in west side of the meadow. Gran got word to our kin and late one moonless night they came and dug up Ma. They built a huge funeral pyre in hills to give Ma a proper sendoff."

Tears rolled down Nadine' face as she looked to her Pa for answers. "That true Pa? You killed Ma?"

Pa slumped in the chair, burying his face in his hands. "Ah hell, it's true, girl. And there ain't a day goes by that I don't regret what I did. But she wasn't takin' you and Carl to live with those heathens.' He reached for the jug and took a drink.

Nadine looked to Carl and started to cry. He went to her side, wrapping his arm around her shoulders. "Go pack the things you can't live without…I'll be waiting right here for you," Carl said. A few minutes later Nadine returned to the parlor wearing her Ma's favorite dress and a carrying a small bag of her belongings. "I'm ready, Carl. Let's go," she said placing a rope around Blu's neck to keep him close.

Carl smiled, taking his sister's hand as they walked out the door stopping only to grab his shotgun and his belongings he'd left on the stoop. They walked out to the meadow and up into the hills in silence.

Desolation Blues

I am old, I am tired
As I walk through these millenniums
Of love and laughter
Of failures and disappointments
I have watched the rise and fall
Of emotions
Dreamed delusions of grandeur
Walked in the fields of adoration
And witnessed the downfall of my being
Visions have passed before the
Panoramic screen within my brain
Only to be shattered
Time and time again
By fear and diffidence
Once upon a time
The universe was mine to behold
Yet slipped through my fingers
Leaving me an empty shell
Passing among the multitudes
Like a ghost.

Magic Charm

When the leaves rustle on the
Autumn winds
I call to the spirits to send
To me the one
I was destined to love
One who will
Love and cherish only me
I harken thee spirits of the past
Send to me on the chill winds
As the stars twinkle above
The one I'm destined to love
And spend eternity with.

Solitaire

I am me
And nothing more
If that you cannot accept
Then leave me be in solitude

The Witch's Familiar

The familiar laid upon his perch watching the fires of Mid-Summer burn high into the sky. He watched his witch laugh and dance around the bonfire enjoying herself. He watched until his eyes grew heavy and he laid back dreaming of his sister. He missed his Snow, wished she was still by his side, how he had loved laying his head on her lush, white fur.

He awoke with a start at the sound of the revelers cheering as someone had leaped over the bonfire as the embers began to die down as sunset approached. He began to clean his ginger fur as he watched his younger sister and baby brother play in the courtyard just beyond the front door. He searched the revelers for his witch and finally saw her kissing a handsome man, who had recently moved into the village. Content all was well in his world he sneaked out the door, past the youngsters to roam the night away. He much preferred the warm breeze of the night winds in summer. He sang the songs of the cat world into the wee hours of the morning.

Before he knew it, Lughnasadh was upon them, the bonfires would soon light up the hillside. The first harvest of the season when the mice began scampering about storing food for the cold months ahead. They were a little slower with all the weight they greedily put on as they roamed the fields. He caught a mouse with ease for his dinner and another to bring to his witch. He quietly entered the cottage, as the moon rose high in the sky, his witch was writing a spell in the candle light. He jumped upon the table and placed his gift before her. She looked up and said, "Thank you, my love. That's a nice plump one indeed." He sat down and began cleaning his cleaning his face as he watched her work. He knew she never ate his gifts but it made him feel special when she praised him for the gift. He thought his witch was beautiful, he never tired of studying her face; he liked to put his paw on her high cheek bones. She in turn would tell him what a handsome little man he was.

As the years passed he watched over his witch, helping to weave her spells and hex those who had come into her disfavor. He did his best to teach the younger cats the ways of a witch's cat, although he was not sure how much they really paid a mind to. He knew his younger sister, who his witch named for the color of a fruit would someday take his place and would be even more powerful than him. He wondered about his little brother but took solace in the fact his witch named him after what the magic they made; someday he'd live up to his name. At night he lay weaving spells of his own as he slept, most were to keep to him, the younger cats and his witch safe. He always made a point of sleeping between her and the door when she slept, guarding what was his. He often found himself casting a spell to see how his sister fared in the Summerland, he missed her so much. Sometimes he awoke to help his witch cast her magic into the witching hour as she wove her spells into the stars above. He loved those quiet imes in the early morning hours when it was just him and his witch. She never failed to thank him for his help. She quietly rewarded him with a treat from her sparse meal. He loved a bite or two of sweet pastry she baked upon the old cook stove. And on rare days a bit of chicken she had cooked. She stroked his fur and told him what good little man he was to help and protect her. He twitched his tail, in long sweeping strokes. He was content, his witch was happy and the youngsters were settling down to learn more from him. The familiar's tail twitched as he watched over his loved ones.

The seasons passed, the witch's Wheel of the Year turned and old age had crept up, the years were starting to take their toll. He felt his magic fading, but as long as his heart beat he would help his witch weave her biding. Some days it was hard to jump upon the work table, his joints grown stiff with the years, his witch would lift him up and stroke his fur, telling him what a good familiar he has been; his heart would soar and he would purr as he rubbed his head against her cheek. She smiled and watched as he began to work his magic into her spell.

He found the more the Wheel of the Year turned he was simply content to lay on his perch watching his younger sister help his witch. He beamed with joy when she would tell little sis "Your brother taught you well." His tail would twitch with contentment knowing he had pleased his witch.

His favorite time of year approached, Samhain, when the ancestors visited and his Snow came to see him. He hoped he'd see it another year. But if he didn't he would be satisfied with a life well lived having served his witch and having taught the ones who would will fill his void. The familiar laid upon his perched like a sentinel, watching his witch until his eyes grew heavy; his tail slowly, contentedly, twitched.

Tyme

Chattering beyond the wind
Beckoning Tyme to come
To the mountain
Begging Tyme to fall
Upon her knees
To whisper to the everlasting Eve
To bare all that rips apart her soul To make the sacrifice to the God's
Of old, the path of the ancient ones
Tyme cover your ears drown out the rivers
And the tears of sage's before
Bury your head beneath the thorns and willows
Hide your body in fields Beneath mother earth's greenery
Stretch upon the Pebble strewn beaches
While the sea Embraces your sorrows
And cries to the sirens who swim the ocean depths
To wash your sins Climb stealthily across the foothills to the highest peaks
As the stars twinkle down from above
Lady moon smiles gently soothes, strengthens, renews
As Tyme listens to the ancients
Chatter beyond the winds
Sharing secrets of the old ways
Beckoning Tyme to embrace
The other worldly musings.

Ghost Ships

Ghost ships on the horizon
Gently rocking
On the silver waves
In the moonlight
Wind whistling through the sails
Whispering of ages gone by.

SHATTERED

In the evening
When the twilight
Turns to night
Loneliness slips
Through the cracks
Of the threshold of my mind
The old hallow ache
Creeps through my soul
And that hole in my heart deepens.
The blackness turns into
The wee hours of the morn
As ghosts of hidden realities
Emerge from behind closed doors
Awaking me from a fitful slumber
And the time we shared forever vanished
Your face blurs in my mind
Lost in deep with the embers of your funeral pyre
That now lay cold and mangled
In eternal darkness.

Dust in the Wind

Branches scrapped at the windows in the wind. Aramis stirred in his chair, the room was growing cold now that the fire had gone out and he'd fallen asleep listening to the rain fall upon the roof of the small barren cottage. He rose slowly, his old bones creaking, protesting the cold with each movement. The thunder echoed through the fairy compound setting his nerves on edge. He went to the window looking out into the garden as the lightning flashed, striking a statue in the garden. He could see no movement in court yard, he pulled his cloak tightly around himself wondering how long he'd slept. The lightning struck the tiny hill where Bilbo, Lara and Sasha were buried, Aramis jumped away from the window, his heart pounding wildly as the thunder boomed and reverberated through the valley. He began to pace restlessly about the room trying to decide whether to venture out into the rain to find someone or stay where he was out of the storm and wait for them to find him. Suddenly he felt very alone but he refused to believe Kailen would forget him; leave him behind to die alone. He walked through the empty rooms of his cottage one last time making sure he'd not left anything of importance behind. At last he stopped at the fire place resting his achy foot on the hearth he felt a stone shift beneath his boot. He knelt down and pried the stone away, he pulled something out of the hiding spot wrapped in a velvet cloth. He smiled as he pulled the cloth away revealing a small box made of polished oak. A tear rolled down his graying cheek as he wondered how he'd almost left his treasure behind. He opened the box; it smelled of frankincense and myrrh a small piece of last year's Yule log lay inside. Lara had given him the box shortly after Bilbo had died. Bilbo had treasured the little box all his life.

Suddenly the door burst open, Bram stomped into the room rain dripping from his cloak. "Lord Aramis," he said, "We have been looking all over for you."

"Yes, I came in here to see if I'd forgotten anything and I'm afraid I fell asleep."

"Kailen sent us to find you. Lord Aramis we need to be on our way before the mists close over the pass and the land of Fey is lost forever." Aramis took one final look at the room and put the box in the pocket of his cloak as Bram took his arm they dashed out into the rain and into the Great Hall. He stopped looking about the room, Kailen had ordered all the candles lit one last time, it had never looked lovelier or lonelier than it did at this moment.

"Lord Aramis, hurry! Your carriage is waiting we must be on the road. We are the last to leave." Aramis looked around the room one last time wishing there were time to play one last song and ran out into to his carriage. Bram closed the door and motioned to the driver. "Hold tight we'll be moving fast."

Aramis watched as Bram swung up on his horse, heading the horse for the mountains and giving him his head. He sat watching out the window saying a silent good bye to the beautiful old village he had lived in since his sixteenth year, his heart hurt knowing he'd never see it again. The lightning struck nearby as the thunder rolled off the steep mountainside, he pulled the leather curtain down, fastening it securely to keep out the rain. He leaned back into the seat, pulling the warm blankets around him to ward off the cold night air and closed his eyes cherishing each memory rolling across his mind of the years in the compound.

It was a time in the Land of Fey when the darkness was overpowering the light, when magic was growing dim the time of man was dawning to reign over the land. The signs of change had been subtle at first, so minuet few noticed the darkness slowly etching over the land. With each turning of the Wheel of the Year Kailen's prophecies proved to be true and even the most skeptical had started to pay heed to his visions.

Aramis was escorted to Kailen's chambers in the wee hours of the morning. He was beyond irritated with having been awoken at such a ghastly hour. He stomped into Kailen's bed chamber, "You summoned me, my lord," he said sarcastically as he bowed.

"Lord Aramis, you never fail to amuse, even in the darkest hours," Kailen said smiling, despite the worry written all over his face.

Aramis watched him for a moment then said, "Kailen, I apologize, I was irritated being woken up in the middle of the night. What is the matter?"

"I have just had another dream," Kailen said pouring them each a goblet of watered-down wine. "Our world is changing, one day the Land of Fey will be forgotten, banished and the religion of man will take over the land and we will have become but a myth."

Aramis stood in silence sipping his drink. At last he said, "Kailen, are you sure your dreams are true?"

Kailen sat down with sigh and motioned for Aramis to join him. "Yes, the dreams are vivid and true, they have become more intense since Bilbo's death, with each passing full moon they grow stronger, more foreboding."

"We have always lived in the shadows beyond the mists," Aramis said. "How can the darkness come to be our enemy?"

"No, you are wrong there, Aramis. We have not always lived beyond the mists. There was a time when man and fairy lived and fought side by side, it is a time long gone and nearly forgotten except for the songs of the bards. We we're not hidden in the mists; we walked from sunrise to sunset together and time was not suspended as we know it today. We worshiped our Gods and Goddesses freely, in harmony." Aramis took a deep breath, opened his mouth to speak but thought better of it and sat in silence watching Kailen pace about the room.

"Our race ages more slowly than the human," Kailen continued at last, "We live for millenniums while the human is confined to decades; it has always been so. It was not until the first human joined with a fairy in marital coupling that the dark veils were weaved between the Fey and Man. The Gods and Goddesses were angered with the union in my great-great grandfathers time. King Avery was so enamored with a beautiful human girl he planned to make her his wife at the mid-summer festival. The old ones railed against the union; told him it was forbidden for Fey to marry human. They told him he could keep her as his consort but the Fey blood must remain pure. The King did not listen and passed over a fairy Princess for the girl. Things did not go well for the old King and his bride; she could not conceive an heir and left him for a younger human in the end. Not long after the first warning of the dark times starting coming in dreams to the elders, slowly the mists began to swirl about separating the Fey from the human landscape. The years passed into my father's time when King Brokk met a human named Holly, the two fell madly in love. He kept her hidden in a small hamlet where he visited her for months on end. He paid little heed to the warnings of the past and when Holly was with child he doted on her endlessly. She died in child birth one rainy night as the lightning flashed and the thunder boomed in the sky. The Gods were not pleased, as punishment they pushed the Land of Fey farther into the mists. They decreed that any human could enter our boundaries, they could stay as long as they wanted but once they returned to the other world they would age according to the time they had spent here, what they perceived as hours here was in reality was years in the human realm. Many had stayed so long when they stepped outside the mists they turned to dust within minutes." Kailen paused, motioning to the serving girl to fill their glasses with fresh wine.

Aramis sat quietly sipping the wine trying process all Kailen had told him. "So both Fairy and Man are responsible for the coming of the dark time?"

"Yes, it is so. One without the other could not have displeased the Gods so. Kailen looked away. "The third and final warning came when Queen Shea became enamored with Rhys. She had done her duty to King Orin, bore him two Princes and a Princess, she had seen Rhys from afar for years. Then one mid-summer eve she called to him from the mists, he left his wife and unborn child behind for a life with Shea. The old King looked the other way for years but eventually his jealousy of the younger man got the best of him and he ordered Shea to set aside her lover and return to his side. Shea refused. King Orin decreed she'd not be welcome at his palace until she gave up Rhys or he died. She laughed and scandalously continued her affair with Rhys. When Orin was upon his death bed Shea returned to the palace and took her rightful place as Queen. King Orin had barely been dead a month when she moved Rhys into the palace. She and Rhys never married but Shea bore him a son. It appeared to all that she had the God's favor until the boy's eighth year when he died from a fall from his horse. Things were never the same between Rhys and Shea after that, they argued and Rhys threatened to cross the mists. Years later in one of his fever fugues he made his way to the borders trying to get back home. Shea had followed him on horseback and watched from the shadows with tears in her eyes as he turned to dust in the moonlight."

"That is when the haunting dreams began?" Aramis whispered.

"Yes, I was just a boy then and the dreams only came from time to time. I did not understand what they meant. My father warned me that one day the dreams would be all too clear. He said I would be the one to lead our people to a new haven. It was not until after Bilbo died that I began to see what he had told me." He sighed long and hard as if he'd just let a weight off his weary shoulders. "Aramis, my friend, I need you to help me. There is so much that needs be done before the time of man comes to be. I need to know I can count on you."

Aramis stared at Kailen then finally said, "Of course, my lord, I will do all I can."

"Good I hoped I could count on you." Kailen let out another long sigh. He called to have plate of food brought to them and handed Aramis another drink. "No one lives forever, not you nor I; some of us live longer than most but nothing is forever."

Aramis went back to his cottage as the sun rose in the eastern sky. He paced about the sitting room, his mind reeling from all that Kailen had told him. At long last he sat down at his writing to outline Kailen's plan and began to write down his plans to carry out his part of the prophecy.

As the years passed he searched through every hamlet in the forest kingdom looking for those creatures with a flair for the dramatic who would learn the tales handed down through the generations who he and Kailen could entrust with title of Bard. One by one he brought his students to the Fey compound to learn the tales and songs.

At times he felt over-whelmed with this urgent duty, but when felt himself sinking into despair he remembered Kailen's words. 'Someday a king will be born again who will be strong enough to unchain the magic and set the Land of Fey free. He will weave new tales for the bards to sing praise, until that day we must be content with preserving our history and bring the prophecies to life.'

Bram yelled, startling Aramis from his thoughts as the driver urged the horses on, faster and faster. The lightning struck behind the carriage and the thunder boomed, the sound resonating from the mountain walls. He pulled the blankets tighter, his breath caught in his throat as the carriage tilted onto two wheels when they rounded a curve. He wanted to open the leather flap on the window but was too afraid to move, too afraid what he might see when the lightning illuminated the land.

The lightning struck again at the crown of the pass, boulders began to fall on the road behind them, the thunder boomed one deafening crash after another then silence. The carriage began to slow as caught up to the others and stopped.

"Bram?" one of the riders called out.

"Yes. Kai. We are here."

"Thank the Gods and Goddesses," Kai said. "We were not sure if you would make it when we heard all the commotion on the pass."

"It was close, my friend, we made it just in time. There was a moment just before we crested the mountain I thought we would have to abandon the wagon and ride the horses to safety. But thanks to Hale expertly urging the horses over the muddy road we were just ahead of the chaos that reigned down from above. The God's were truly looking out for us in spite of their fury."

"Kailen will be relieved to know you safe." Kai said. "I will send word ahead with a rider."

Aramis peered around Bram looking back up the road. The only sound was from the rain pouring steadily over the land. "Shall we take a look, Lord Aramis? I am curious, too. They walked up the slippery road, the night air became dense, almost stifling. They came to an abrupt halt as the road seemed to disappear into nothingness and the coal, black mists swirled; it was obvious there was nothing beyond the pitch-black night before them. The Land of Fey as was sealed away from the time of man.

Aramis leaned into Bram at the stark realization. "Are you alright, my Lord?"

"I think so." he said in a small voice. "It is one thing to hear the details of a vision but quite a different matter when it comes to be."

"Indeed my Lord," Bram put his hand on Aramis' shoulder. "Had we been one moment slower we would have been locked out of Fairyland forever."

"Locked in that void of nothingness I'm afraid, Bram." Aramis took a deep breath; the air had grown stagnant. "I wonder how many didn't make it?"

“My Lord, let’s walk back to the carriage,” Bram said. “There were those who chose to stay behind.”

“What will become of them?” Aramis whispered.

Bram looked up the hill and back to Aramis. “They will fall asleep and wake up mortal. They are the ones who will make us legends.” The rain began to pour harder. “Come Aramis, we need to catch up with the rest of the caravan. I will escort you back up here once we are settled in if you want.”

Aramis looked into the darkness, pulling his cloak tight. “No Bram, I do not think I’ll ever want to come back up here. That part of us is gone forever, but a memory.”

“As you wish, I only thought you might want to see it in the light of day.”

“Thank you, Bram,” Aramis whispered. “But the light of day will never shine on this road again.” He looked into the darkness one more time then stepped into his carriage. His heart felt as cold and heavy as the black barrier standing between the worlds.

Bram urged the horses on slowly as the carriage began to slip in the mud. The rain continued to pour, running down the road and hillside into the valley and river below. He feared the road would wash out before them and they would be forced to leave the wagons behind until the God’s fury ended. Slowly, steadily they wound down the slippery road. Lightning continued to strike around them and the thunder crashed but the rage was not nearly fierce. The God’s and Goddesses were growing tired. Appeased the Land of Fey was sealed away.

They heard shouting as they rounded the long sweeping curve that led into the valley. Bram rode ahead to see what was going on. He feared the worst; a wagon wheel had come off or worse someone was hurt in their haste to get to their new home. He abruptly reigned in his horse and sat staring at the vision before him. He smiled as the weary travelers rejoiced at the sight of their new home. His stallion began to paw at the muddy ground impatiently before Bram turned back towards the wagons. He grabbed the reigns of a horse being led down the mountainside and headed back to Aramis.

"Lord Aramis," he shouted as he neared the carriage. "Lord Aramis."

"Yes, yes I hear you, Bram. What seems to be the matter?"

"Are you up to a ride?" Bram said as he dismounted and reached to open the door of the carriage.

"Goodness what has you all fired up?"

"You'll see. Shall I help you mount?" Bram said excitedly.

"I suppose but can't it wait until the carriage gets me there?"

"I will be sometime before the wagons make their way down the road. This is something you'll want to see now."

"Alright then let me gather my things..."

"No, leave your things we will unload what you need for the night once the wagons get to the compound."

"Very well, let me get my walking stick." Aramis said.

Bram brought the mare over to the carriage door and pushed her close so Aramis could mount easily. He mounted his horse and motioned to Aramis to take the lead. Some minutes later Aramis slowed the horse, his mouth fell open and his eyes grew wide. He reigned in the mare and starred at the sight before him. He marveled at the magnificent village before him, rising high into the mountain, illuminated with the light from thousands of candles and lanterns in every window and doorway. Lanterns lined the river in front of the massive compound that of mortar and bricks rising high into the heavens kissing the mountain side as far as the eye could see. Lightning still struck all the higher peaks and the thunder rolled off the mountain echoing through the valley. Tears began roll to stream down Aramis' cheek.

Bram urged his horse closer. "Is it not grand, my Lord Bard?"

Aramis continued to look at the lights, listening to the delighted cries from those rounding the curve. He swallowed hard and found his voice, "Indeed, Bram, indeed it is. Did you know it would be so huge?"

"No, not in my wildest dreams. Kailen promised the first glimpse would be a sight to behold."

"It is a sight to behold." Bram said.

"It is magnificent." Aramis said. "How did he manage to pull this off?"

"Workers have been creating his visions ever since that night he called you to his chambers..." said Bram.

"Yes, yes I know that," Aramis broke in. "How did he manage to create this vision of light before us?"

"The Fey from all over began migrating to this valley through the dreams. Kailen sent word ahead with our fastest riders to have the compound bathed in light for a fortnight to welcome all who found their way."

"Are we the last to arrive?

"Yes, Kailen waited until the last possible moment to leave to grant your request for one last Mabon celebration in the old compound," Bram said.

"Did I put anyone in danger with my request?" Aramis said.

"My Lord, Kailen would not have allowed our wish had he thought we would not make it. Now come Kailen is waiting for us in the great hall," Bram said.

"Tell me true, Bram, were you afraid we would get struck in the black void between the worlds?"

Bram hesitated. "I will not lie there was a couple moments I thought we would be in that blackness forever."

Aramis shifted uncomfortably in the saddle and urged the mare forward. "Thank you for your honesty, Bram."

"My Lord," Bram lowered his head as Aramis rode on in silence. Bram urged his horse up beside Aramis as they road through the compound gates. They stopped in the great courtyard taking in the beauty of their new home. Bram dismounted and led the mare to the mounting block so Aramis could dismount with ease. He motioned to a servant to help Aramis get down the steps and handed the Aramis his walking stick. "Go on to the hall, Aramis. I'll be there as soon as I find out which cottage is yours and find someone to unload your bed and have it set up by the time you are ready to retire."

"Do not be long, Bram. I would like you at my side," Aramis said.

"I will be as quick as I can." He bowed and turned, shouting orders as he led the horses to the stable.

Aramis followed the servants to the Great Hall. He stopped outside the doors straightening his clothes, hoping he didn't look as disheveled as he felt. He took a deep breath and entered the hall; he was bathed in the golden warmth of the candle light of the chandeliers and the candelabras placed about the room. For the first time since he had become a Bard he did not care about making a grand entrance; he only wanted to get to his chair at Kailen's table. He nodded to familiar faces and greeted those he knew by name as he slowly made his way across the room.

"Aramis," Kailen said. "Come have seat and some wine. I am so glad you made it over the pass in time. I was worried."

Aramis limped over to his chair and sat down before answering. "There were moments we all wondered, my Lord, but Bram pushed hard until we got over the pass to safety." He reached for a goblet and greedily drank from it as Bram put his hand on Aramis' shoulder and sat down on the chair beside him. Aramis raised his goblet to Bram and motioned for more wine.

Bram smiled. "It is alright, my Lord, we are home."

"Yes. Yes we are." Aramis looked about the room at all the unfamiliar faces and those he'd known all his life. He let out a long sigh and leaned back into his chair. The Fey had come from near and far to settle in this new land; he was looking forward to talking with all of them and dreading it at the same time.

It was near dawn when Bram escorted Aramis to his new cottage. It was lined on one side by the garden and the other side the mountains reaching to the heavens. The river below shimmered in the moon light as it flowed through the valley towards the sea. Aramis yawned. "Sleep well, old friend," Bram said. "I have ordered a warm bath drawn for you and your bed awaits."

"Thank you," he said. "For everything…not just tonight but through all the years, you are a good friend. Sleep well."

"A couple hours and I will be back up to supervise the unloading of your wagons. We'll try not to wake you."

"You need your rest too, Bram."

"Don't worry I will sleep well tomorrow." He bowed and smiled at Aramis before he headed to his quarters.

Aramis awoke with a start his room was dark and hot; someone had placed a dark cloth over his window to blackout the sunlight. He listened for a few minutes as the workers brought his belongings into the cottage then rolled over and went back to sleep.

Over the next few weeks he did little more than sleep and instruct the workers where to place things around the cottage. He would go for long walks along the river, sometimes he would walk up the steep, winding paths in the mountain and look down on the wonderous compound he now called home. Occasionally he would dine in the great hall at the evening meal but mostly he would ask for a tray to be sent to his cottage saying only he didn't feel well. He read every night and composed songs and poems but had not performed since they arrived in the new land.

Bram became worried and went to check on his old friend several times day. Aramis seemed genuinely pleased to see him but Bram sensed a deep sadness beneath the old fox's smile. Kailen requested he recite a poem or sing a song after the evening meal on several occasions but Aramis declined saying he was too tired to do a song justice and would disappear from the great hall yet late at night a haunting melody would drift over the compound as Aramis played his mandolin. Kailen began to see Bram's concern for the Bard was more than just adjusting to their new home; he was brooding over something he wasn't sharing with anyone.

Kailen ordered a grand meal to be prepared, inviting all to come to celebrate the Fey's new home in this wonderous valley. Bram knocked on Aramis' door promptly at 8 o'clock to escort him to the meal. Aramis answered the door in his robe, holding sheets of paper in one paw and a quill in the other. "My lord, you are not ready for the meal."

"I'm afraid I have lost track of time, Bram. I have been writing most of the day," Aramis said absently, returning to his writing table.

"Come let me help you get ready," Bram said heading to the bedchamber.

"Please send my apologies to Kailen. Tell him I am not feeling all that well."

"Lord Aramis, that is a lie and you know it." Bram said.

Aramis looked up from writing. Threw his quill on table splattering ink all over his paper as he stood. "How dare you talk to me in that manner!"

Bram laughed. "So there is still some spunk in you" Let me help you..."

"No," Aramis broke in. "I do not feel well and Kailen will have to accept that."

"I am sorry Aramis but I have instructed to bring you to dinner and if you wish to attend in your robe so be it. Kailen has ordered your presence and you are going, even if I have to carry you."

Aramis glared at Bram. "Very well, since I have been ordered like a commoner." He stomped dramatically into his bed chamber, pour me a glass of brandy and one for yourself while I dress. C'este des conneries!"

Bram smiled as he listened to drawers and doors being slammed while Aramis decided what to wear as he continued to cuss in French, calling Kailen the most unflattering things he could think of. At last he emerged from his room dressed in his signature thigh-high boots, velvet britches and a brocade coat, which Kailen had given him last Yule.

He bowed as he entered the sitting room. Bram laughed as he handed him the brandy. “To you, my lord.” Aramis downed the glass and pored another for them both.

Aramis entered the great hall and exaggeratedly bowed to Kailen before heading to his seat at the royal table. Bram bowed and grinned at Kailen’s feeble attempt to keep from laughing. “Aramis I am so happy you have joined us in this celebration,” Kailen held up his wine glass in toast to the Bard. “Now let us eat.” He signaled to have dinner served.

After several hours of feasting and drinking along with endless speeches Aramis yawned, hoping to make his escape. He waited until Kailen appeared in deep conversation then rose to leave. Kailen watched his bard walk quickly through the crowd, let him think he had escaped another night of performing before he called out. “LordBard, won’t you grace us with a song?”

Aramis stopped, debating whether to pretend ha had not heard Kailen over the crowd and continue out the door or answer his King. He turned to Kailen and bowed. ‘My Lord.”

“We have not been graced by voice your since we arrived, Lord Bard. Will you sing us a song?”

“I am afraid feel a bit light headed, Kailen. I wish to go back to my quarters and lay down.”

“Come here Aramis. I wish a word,” Kailen said sternly. Aramis lowered his head and headed back to the table.

“Lord Bard you have had one excuse after another for months now to get out performing. I understand you are at loose ends, we all are, your songs and stories would go far to ease the minds of everyone and put some normalcy back in our lives. You are the Royal Bard and you will play the harp and sing, perhaps recite a few poems or a tale or two of our history. I am counting on you to cheer up everyone. I will not except any more excuses.”

Aramis looked about the great hall, it looked exactly like the one they had left behind. He looked into the faces anxiously awaiting a song. “Kailen, I have nothing prepared…”

Kailen cut him off, in a low angry voice he said, "You will perform, Aramis. I order it."

"As you wish, my Lord." Aramis bowed and walked to the center of the hall where the harp waited, its strings glittering, bathed in the candle light. He sat before the grand harp and lovingly ran his finger tips across the polished frame. The harp began to hum lowly, awaiting the commands, he began to pluck the strings, inviting them to sing his emotions as he nimbly stroked their shimmering chords. Nearly an hour later he arose from his seat as the last note echoed through the hall and bowed. When he looked up he saw everyone standing and applauding, calling for more. Tears rolled down his cheeks as he turned and bowed to Kailen. He stepped away from the harp and started for the door, he felt a strong hand on his shoulder as Bram guided him through the hall into the garden and the cool night air. They walked in silence to his front door and Aramis bid his friend goodnight.

"It has been a good night, Lord Bard, sleep well." Bram smiled and bowed.

Aramis stood quietly at his window watching young lovers stroll through the garden, sharing kisses full of promises on their way home. He sat before his fireplace, sipping another brandy before heading to his bed, not even bothering to undress. He fell asleep the minute his head hit the pillow dreaming of his wife, Serene, his only true love.

He awoke late in the morning he had not intended to sleep so long but this was the first time he had slept so peacefully since the move. He felt content having dreamed of sweet Serene. He thought back to his performance, he had not realized until the moment he touched the harp just how much he needed to fulfill his duties as Royal Bard. He loved and hated Kailen for forcing him to perform. He laughed as he looked down at his boots, he could not remember the last time he had fallen asleep with all his clothes on. He pulled his boots off and ordered a bath before heading to the great hall to eat.

Fruits, bread and cheese and watered-down wine had been set out for a late morning snack. He filled his plate and poured a goblet of wine. He headed towards the garden to enjoy the sunshine while he ate.

"Lord Bard, a word with you," Kailen said.

Aramis jumped, he not expected to see anyone this time of day, especially not Kailen. "But of course, my liege," he bowed his head, "Can we talk here in the garden?"

"Of course we can. And let us dispense with the formalities and sarcasm, my old friend," Kailen said motioning to the serving girl to follow them with his plate. "I want to thank you for last night's performance." They sat in silence as Aramis ate, savoring each bite. At last he said, "Aramis what is the matter? I know are unsettled here in our new home as we all are. I do not understand why you keep to yourself, refuse to fulfill your duties as Royal Bard."

Aramis sighed and took a long drink of wine. "Kailen, it is not that I do not care, I just worry I made the wrong decision coming here."

"How so?" Kailen said as leaned forward in his chair.

"I left all those I loved behind, Bilbo, Lara and Serene, I out lived all my children, left all their children's children behind. I am not there to watch over Bilbo's, Lara's and Serene's graves or those of my children. There is no going back to them and it eats away at my soul." He looked away as the tears flowed freely down his almost white cheeks.

Kailen sat in silence watching his friend, he had been so preoccupied over the years with the burden of the dreams he had not noticed the fox had aged so much. He felt sad life had passed by without his noticing. At last he said, "Aramis come with me. I wanted this to be a surprise at Samhain but I can see you need it now." He motioned to a serving boy, instructing him to send for Bram as they began to walk towards the far side of the compound. Bram caught up as they started up the winding path, taking hold of Aramis' arm.

Aramis smiled. "Thank you, Bram. I was not planning on a hike. I forgot my walking stick." Bram smiled back, guiding Aramis up the step path to where Kailen waited.

"Is it not beautiful?" Kailen said, looking over the valley below.

Aramis' breath caught in his throat as he looked upon the lush valley with the dark crystal river winding through the plain, running to the blue ocean beyond. Rays of sunlight beamed golden warmth across the beauty before him.

"I built this place for all to come to honor their loved ones who have passed to the other side. Everyone is welcome here," Kailen said.

"It is beautiful, my Lord. I cannot find the words…"

"Come let me show you the rest."

Aramis hesitated then followed. The path turned into a garden lined with flowers and statuaries were decorated with symbols and candles dotted the plateau hidden in the cliffs rising high above them. Kailen continued through a doorway in the mountain motioning for them to follow. Bram led Aramis slowly into the chamber, the walls were lined with sandstone and crystals; candles bathed the chamber. Many hallways lead deep within the mountain from the outer chamber. Kailen started down a dimly lit passageway to an inner room. He grabbed several candles from the stand by the door and began to light them, he handed one to Aramis and then to Bram as they entered the tiny room. "Look around, Aramis" Kailen said as he lit the candles in the room.

Aramis walked around the room running his paws over the paintings and trinkets placed around the room. In the far corner were two tiny tombs of alabaster with the names Bilbo and Lara carved in bold fairy lettering. He walked to the opposite side of the room where Serene's tomb stood. He began to cry as he ran his hand over the cold alabaster.

"I had them moved here years ago. Aramis…" he paused, searching for the right words. "Part of the prophecy was to build a memorial to house the Kings and Queens, the warriors who forged our land and the Bards…"

"Have a seat Aramis," Bram said guiding him to the bench by the door. "You look a bit shaky."

"Yes, thank you, Bram," he said. He sat letting out a mournful sigh. "Kailen how, when did you do this?"

"As soon as it was decided this word be the site of our new home. I instructed my men to find the most lovely spot here to build the memorial. First the workers, began by leveling the land for the garden and as the visions progressed they dug into the hillside carving out chambers to house the ashes and bodies of our ancestors. He walked about the room, smelled the freshly cut flowers before continuing. "Do you remember when I had the flowers dug up on the hill, only to replace them with more flowers? It was a ruse. Late one night I had each coffin dug up and brought here to their final rest, in a tomb of alabaster."

Aramis sat in silence gathering the words to speak. "Then all these years I have been worrying over empty graves?

"Yes, I am afraid it is so. But it is who and what those tiny graves represented that mattered."

"What about those who are left in the outer world? Those who make the pilgrimage each spring to pay respects to Bilbo?"

"The graves, the burial stones are still there, they represent everything Bilbo stood for along with Lara's dreams and those of Serene, that was not taken away from them. Lord Bard, I meant this as a surprise on Samhain but you have been so distraught, I had to unveil it to you today."

"I do not know what to say, Kailen," Aramis said. He looked about the chamber.

"Someday Aramis you will sleep beside Serene," Kailen pointed to the unmarked tomb beside her, "Just as I will sleep beside my dear Annabeth in a room off the oratory. Come Bram, let us give Aramis some time to himself."

Bram stepped towards the door and put his hand on the Bard's shoulder. "My Lord are you alright?"

"Yes, I am," he said. "Bram don't go too far…"

"I won't, I'll be in the garden," Bram said. He lingered for a moment watching the fox then headed out to the garden.

"Lord Bard, Samhain is less than a week away, I expect a special song about this," Kailen said as he turned to leave Aramis to his thoughts.

"You will have it, my King," Aramis said as he looked at Serene's tomb. "I have been preparing for this Year's celebration for months."

He sat for a time looking at the tombs of those he loved, he was in awe that Kailen had brought his loved ones to the new home without anyone in the outer world having a clue. He rose slowly looking from tomb to the other. He walked to Bilbo's then Lara's likeness tracing their images with his finger tips. He smiled sadly as he moved to Serene's tomb. "My love, it has been so long," he whispered. "No wonder the dreams of you have been so vivid again." He caressed her image her image lovingly. "I wish you could have lived to your sons and daughters grow up. I wish you were still by my side to see this new land..." he began to cry; his heart grew heavy.

Samhain was revered with the solemn rituals, the telling of the ancient ones, praise for their new home remembrance of loved ones and the unveiling of the memorial garden and burial chambers hidden within the mountain. Aramis recited poems and songs accompanying himself on the harp and mandolin. He ended his part of the celebration with a benediction filled references to the past with promises of hope for the future. The feasting and merriment lasted through the night until the bonfires began to burn out around dawn.

The seasons passed as the Wheel of the Year turned marking the passing of the years. Aramis' fur had turned almost completely silver, he had slowed down, handing many of his duties over to his apprentice, a pretty young fairy named Eria. She had been orphaned when she was but a babe and lived with Bram and his wife but spent most of days learning all that Aramis had to teach.

Aramis sang a song or recited a poem each night after dinner, his need for performing never slowed. He had found a new burst of creativity that filled the hours he was alone in this cottage yet the years were beginning to take their toll, just as it did with all who shared the fairy blood but had not been born Fey. For the first time since Serene's death he felt truly content and happy.

Bram worried about his old friend, knew he often missed meals and was growing absent minded. He had long wanted to ask the Bard to come live with him and his wife but didn't want to intrude upon his independence. As the sun rose high in the sky before the Mabon celebration he knocked on the fox's door. Aramis greeted him warmly. After an hour of conversation and a few goblets of watered-down wine Bram said, "I worry about you living by yourself in this cottage."

Aramis sat in silence for a moment before answering, "How so, Bram? I am happy, I am creating new works, I..."

Bram broke in. "Aramis I know you perform nearly every night but you miss meals, you often become confused where you are when you are out walking, I worry about you."

"I am afraid it is part of aging," Aramis said, looking to his writing table.

"Yes, Aramis it is. But you spend too much time alone in this cottage."

"I am always busy, Bram."

"Perhaps," he said looking about the room trying to find the right words. "Aramis I would like you to consider moving into my home. My wife adores you and would welcome the company when I am gone on the King's business. It is time Eria was on her own, she could move into your cottage and you into ours."

"Bram, I appreciate your concern but I am fine."

"You are so stubborn. I have watched you failing for years now, we are all getting older and I would consider it an honor for you to live us."

Aramis looked at the poem he was working on then at Bram, he knew deep down his old friend was right. "Alright Bram, I will accept your generous offer. I know I neglect myself and I would be honored to live in your home."

"You have no idea how happy this makes me." He hugged the old fox.

"Good, let us get through Mabon then I will start packing to move into your home. But right now I need to finish this poem and take a nap before the festivities."

"Yes, as you wish. I'll see you at the Sabbat. We can make plans for your move then." Bram smiled. Aramis watched Bram walk down the path into the garden. He found himself looking forward to living with Bram and his wife.

Aramis woke early from his nap, he bathed and put on his finest clothes for the celebration. The Sabbat would soon start and he wanted to bless the season and recite the new poem before turning the evening over to Eria. He suddenly felt so tired though and sat on the edge of the bed for a few minutes to gather his strength then laid back resting his head on the feather pillow, he closed his eyes and drifted into a deep slumber.

Aramis entered the Great Hall dressed in favorite hat with the purple ostrich plumes, a maroon brocaded jacket, black velvet breaches and soft thigh high leather boots. He walked through the crowd as the music and dancing stopped. The crowd parted and Bilbo came forward to shake his paw, Lara ran to hug him and kiss his cheek. Animal and Fey came forward to greet him as he made his way to the center of the hall. He heard a sweet, lilting, Welsh accent say "Have you forgotten me, my love?" He turned to see Serene waiting in front of the fireplace. He hurried to her side she flung her paws around his neck and kissed him sweetly upon the lips. They began to dance, holding each other tightly as they waltzed into eternity.

PRESENCE

Let my presence be beside you
In the twilight hours
Hear my whispers
As the evening drags endlessly
Alone in your brass bed
Tossing and turning, cold sweat
Beading upon your face
Dreams filled of yesterday
Running and laughing together
Scar the night
Early mourn is here
As you lie awake
Staring at the ceiling as if it might escape
If once more you dare to sleep
With each night and day the
Torment will grow stronger
The pain pulling, ripping
At your mind and soul
The need to tell someone
What you've done driving you mad
Dawn's breaking out there
Dew's sparkling over the field
How we loved that time of morning
When the world began to shake off the darkness
Do you remember?
But we'll never tell
You killed me yesterday.

EYES WIDE SHUT

Shrouded in the dead of night
Silent screams echo through the mists
Lurking like a jilted lover
Hiding in the gloom
Hallow inside, afraidTo live in the light
Too scared to wake in the darkness.
Dreadful secrets haunt, torment
In the inky caverns
Where imaginary demons play
Beckoning to your twisted temptations
Leaving you shuddering, soaked in sweat
Staring into the forbidden
With eyes wide shut.

Midnight Bliss

In the midnight hour
Come to me
As moon rises high
And the moon rises high
Flirt with the moonbeams
My dark lover
Etched in eternal darkness
Your dark kiss
My deliverance, my one desire
I offer you my soul to keep.

Twilight Secrets

The rain began to fall as Nyghtshayd ran through the swirling ground mists, dawn peaked open its sleepy eyes on the horizon bathing the eastern sky in hues of pink and gray. She slipped on the wet leaves blanketing the path to the graveyard, cursing under her breath as she caught herself. She pulled her cloak tight warding off the cold. She was pale and thin, dark circles were etched under her emerald green eyes, aging her well beyond her years. She'd not slept for more than a few hours at time since Fallon's death nearly at fortnight ago.

She'd been up most of the night reading her grandmother's journals searching for answers to better deal with the mob she was about to face. She'd fallen asleep in the wee hours of the morning waking from a fitful slumber to the sounds of voices and horses outside the library window. She closed her eyes for a moment, felt herself drift back to sleep and was startled awake again by the chiming of the old clock in the corner striking the half hour. She jumped up hastily putting on her cloak as she ran out into the cold.

Nyghtshayd paused at the cemetery gates; she could hear men shouting in the distance. She gathered her shirts in her hand and ran to the mausoleum. She could see her uncle Cirrus standing in a wagon barking orders to the men trying to break down the iron gate to the stone building that housed Fallon's casket.

"Uncle Cirrus, stop this madness," she yelled as she neared the wagon. "This is not what I want."

Cirrus climbed from the wagon when he heard her yell wrapping his arms about her thin form. “This is no place for you in your state of mind, niece.” Now go back to Bramble Wood and let us do what needs to be done here.” He motioned for his driver to take her back to the mansion.

“Do not touch me,” she said, shying away from the man. “I am not a child and I will not be treated as one.” “Nyghtshayd, please,” Cirrus reached for her hand. “Just go back home there is work that must be done, the likes of which are not for your eyes.”

“Nonsense, Cirrus, I have heard the rumors about Fallon, the whispers behind my back about him having risen from the grave to roam the night.” She looked upon the men hungry to dispatch her husband’s corpse. “You have no proof it is my husband.”

“Two nights ago the inn keeper in Fall River saw him and just last night the local blacksmith saw him walking down the alley by his shop. Now go home!” His voice rose with anger and he motioned to his driver again.

Nyghtshayd avoided his attempt to grab her, but the man was quicker and stronger. He threw over his shoulder. carried her to Cirrus’ carriage.

They heard a horse coming towards them at a dead gallop and a wagon not far behind, the horses snorting and the jingling harness filled the pale morning air. Jeffery reigned in the fiery stallion, the horse snorted and pawed impatiently at the ground. He looked disapprovingly at the scene playing out before him.

“Let her go,” he barked, reaching for the pistol at his side.

“You over-step your place man servant. Now get off that horse before I have you hanged for horse thievery.” Cirrus turned to the mob smiling. They shouted approval inching closer to the mausoleum entrance eager to finish what they came to do. Jeffery raised his pistol into the air, firing it above the tree line. Silence fell over the crowd.

“Hang me as horse thief would you, you over blown peacock. Fallon released me from my indentured servitude long before his death and Nyghtshayd has given Fallon’s horse to me. I

Carry the papers to prove it and I stay on to watch over her as a friend not a servant." He paused looking out over the faces in the crowd; many had been Fallon's friends. "Do as I say and release her."

The man looked to Cirrus, he nodded. "Let her go." She ran to Jeffery as he dismounted the stallion, he grabbed Nyghtshayd by the waste helping her to quickly mount the horse. He handed her the reins, "If things go bad here ride like the wind to get the sheriff." She nodded.

"Are you daft man putting a frail young woman on a horse like that, in her state of mind? Cirrus blustered to the crowd. Shouts of agreement filled the air as the mob edged forward. Jeffery signaled for his men. They armed themselves with axes, clubs and knives, quickly putting themselves between the crowd and the mausoleum.

A second shot rang out silencing the angry scene; no one had heard the approach of the two riders. The men guided their horses through the crowd to take their place beside Jeffery and Nyghtshayd.

Cirrus broke the silence. "Good morning, Sheriff Stevens, Deputy Terrence..."

"Save the pleasantries, Cirrus, take your men and go home," the Sheriff said. "There'll be no defiling of corpses this morning." Angry shouts rose from the mob, the Sheriff raised his pistol. "Go home," he shouted. "I'll shoot anyone who dares to pass me. Look at yourselves you've turned into a blood thirsty mob over the ramblings of the town drunk. What if it were your kin this mob was trying to defile. Hasn't this woman been through enough with death of her husband? Now go home and sleep it off."

The crowd began to disperse; a few angry shouts rang through the air as they moved away from the mausoleum to the cemetery gates. Jeffery turned to help Nyghtshayd off the horse. She was shaking from the cold, from fear and excitement all at once. She looked gratefully into his eyes, smiling sadly.

He smiled back, reassuringly then said, "You best be hiding that charm."

"Oh, I'd forgotten I'd put it on. It was my grandmother's pentacle." She reached for the necklace holding it lovingly in her hands.

I don't care who it belonged to or if you wear it any more than Fallon did but listen to me girl, hide it in your bodice before someone sees it."

"Jeffery, I..."

"Don't argue with me, hide it," he hissed. "All you need is someone seeing it and accusing you of witchcraft. They'd burn you at the stake and defile Fallon's body for certes. Not even the sheriff would come to your rescue." She felt as though she'd been slapped in the face with his stinging words but deep down knew he was right. "I need a few words with the sheriff," he said. "Instruct the men to tear down the gate."

She watched as he walked away. Jeffery was tall and lean with shoulder length hair he was so much like Fallon. Fallon had always said Jeffery would be there to take care of her no matter what happened. She smiled sadly remembering her husband as she watched the men hitch the team of horses to the iron gate to pull it from its hinges.

In the distance she heard the horses gallop away and felt Jeffery's hand on her shoulder. "You're chilled to the bone," he wrapped a wool blanket around her frail shoulders. "You should go back to Bramble Wood and get into some dry clothes."

"No, I want to see," she said absently watching the men work.

"Be reasonable girl this is no place for you."

"I am no girl. That is my husband's body in there and I will be here to witness what is done today."

Jeffery knew better than to argue with her once her mind was set. The men had lit the torches in the in the mausoleum, she saw them make the sign of the cross. Jeffery placed his hand on her arm as they walked into the tiny dark, cold stone building, the stench of death lingering in the air. The men moved away from the casket as she approached. The lock and the hinges had been broken away from their screws. She ran her fingers along the cold surface of the mahogany box.

"Open it, I want to see," she whispered. She searched the faces of the men standing beside her. "Open it, I want to see," she said louder this time. The men looked to Jeffery. "Don't look to him for orders. Open it."

Jarred out of their indecision the men moved the casket and took off the lid. Nyghtshayd moved forward. Fallon looked as he had the day she buried him in his favorite coat and breeches, his shirt buttoned high and an ascot tied around his neck to hide the gashes in his throat. He looked every bit the way he had 14 days ago except for the fresh mud on his boots. Jeffery leaned over to pull the scarf from Fallon neck, his wounds were healed, no sign of ever having been attacked.

"Nyghtshayd ran her fingers along his chiseled features, cold as alabaster to the touch but recoiled as she traced his lips, still warm and red from feeding. "Leave me," she whispered. She sobbed, long hard gut-wrenching sobs. She could not believe it was true, Fallon had become a monster.

When she came out into the pouring rain Jeffery ran to her taking her in his arms. "Forgive me," she whispered, "I cannot do as I should."

"Go to Bramble Wood and wait," he said. "I'll take care of it."

"No, Jeffery I cannot do it. Chain the coffin, place garlic and hang crosses throughout the mausoleum. Position the coffin so it sits between the two windows so it always has the sun on it. Plant the hawthorn, the wild roses and the mountain ash all around the building. Seal him in his tomb."

"As you wish." he said.

"Jeffery, I need you to go to Bramble Wood and tell my uncle to pack and go home. I'll not tolerate his betrayal. Tell him to be gone by morning. And Jeffery, he's to know nothing of what we found."

In the months following Fallon's death Jeffery watched as Nyghtshayd became more and more reclusive. He followed her every day as she rode to the mausoleum and hid in the shadows as she would sneak out in the dead of night, watching as she hugged the wall that entombed her husband, sobbing uncontrollably. Jeffery pleaded with her to sell Bramble Wood and go to Europe to start her life anew. She agreed, only to relent the next day saying only she couldn't leave.

Finally one sunny afternoon Jeffery could take no more. He grabbed her by the wrists, dragging her to the mirror throwing off the heavy black fabric of mourning. "Look at yourself, Nyghtshayd. He held her tight forcing her to look at her reflection. "Look what your grief has done to you."

She turned away and broke free of his grip. "Why do you do this to me?" she said. "I thought you were here to protect me not torture me."

"Nyghtshayd, you are still young, you have your whole life before you…it is time to let go of this madness and move on. Fallon would not want you to grieve forever."

"Fallon! What would you know of what Fallon wants? He's called to me from his tomb since the beginning. He watches me from the shadows; he speaks to me entreating me to join him in his eternal damnation. I taste his putrid breath upon my lips; feel his deathly embrace as I sleep." She turned away laughing. "Now come here and help me find a spell to break this curse." She pushed one of her grandmother's journals to him. "There has to be something written in these journals to help…"

He pulled her from her chair, forcing her to look at him. "Don't you see there is no spell in those books to break the curse of a vampire? Why are you so obsessed with this nonsense?"

She laughed and pulled the material away from her bodice. The color drained from Jeffery's face, he stumbled backwards. "All these weeks you have been looking at my neck for signs," she laughed. "I knew you suspected; I old Fallon as much, but still he feeds on me."

"How long?" he looked away.

"A month, maybe longer," she said. "He came to me on a moonless night, tricked me, cast a spell upon me."

"There is only one way to dispatch a vampire, I'll gather some men and go to the mausoleum before night fall..."

"It is too late for that, he's no longer there."

Jeffery ran to the stables placing the bridle on his horse and leapt upon his back heading for the cemetery. They thundered through the cemetery gates to the mausoleum. The stallion pawed at the ground nervously as Jeffery inspected the walled-up doorway as they rounded the corner on the west side he saw the broken window. It had been broken from the inside; glass lay in shards on the ground beneath the window frame. He quickly slide off his horse and went to the window to look inside. The chains were broken and casket lid lay where it was thrown across the room. Jeffery cursed as the hawthorn tore at his breeches when he stepped away from the window. He swung easily upon the stallion's back, riding fast to Bramble Wood before darkness fell.

He curried his horse and fed him and the mare a bucket of oats before heading into the house. He entered through the kitchen, he felt uneasy, unsure of what he'd find. He heard voices coming from down the hall. He stopped only to wash up; he was hungry but that would have to wait. As he entered the parlor he saw Nightshayd sitting by the fireplace a glass of brandy in her hand, Fallon was seated across the room from her.

Fallon rose. "Hello, Jeffery. I never thought us to meet again."

"Fallon," Jeffery said hoping his voice didn't betray his false bravado. He walked to the table and poured himself a whiskey downing it in one gulp and poured another. "I'd offer you one but vampires don't drink do they?"

Fallon crossed the room and kissed his wife. "I'll see you later, my dear." He turned to Jeffery and offered his hand. "My dearest friend, thank you for watching over my lovely wife in my absence. I'll leave you two to talk." He walked to the front door.

Jeffery walked to a chair and sat as his knees gave out. He sat staring at Nyghtshayd for a long time before speaking. "Something has changed...what is it?"

"Fallon is going to change me tonight," she smiled sadly at him. "No, do not be alarmed it is what I want. I want to be with my husband." They heard the front door close and Fallon stomp off the porch. "He is gone now, we must talk."

"No! I'll not let it end this way..." Jeffery said.

"Jeffery please listen to me I have so much to say and so little time before he returns. Please promise me you'll do as I ask. No, questions just do as I ask as my dearest friend," she pleaded with her eyes. He sat in silence as she poured another drink for two of them listening to her request.

Jeffery sat watching the fire burn low, Nyghtshayd had long retired to her room waiting for Fallon's return. He sighed heavily; he'd agreed to her last wishes. He poured another drink and had gone into the library instead of his room to wait for the break of day. As he sat on the easy hair he saw the note she'd left for him and the journal. He sat reading her grandmother's journal until dawn. He rose and wiped the tears from his eyes.

As the sun rose in the eastern sky he went to the wood shed and grabbed the axe and wooden stake from the garden. Slowly, cautiously he walked down the steps into the cellar past the casks of brandy and ale to the darkest part of the room where Nyghtshayd had instructed him to go. In the corner was the makeshift coffin where Fallon laid. He opened the coffin lid half expecting Fallon to sit up and chat with him. He stared at his oldest friend for what seemed an eternity before he gathered the courage to pound the stake through his heart. He swung the axe and cut off his former master's head in one swipe, throwing it across the room out of site. Jeffery walked silently up the stairs, tears streaming down his face. He sat down at the kitchen table until the sun began to wane in the western sky.

Just after dusk Jeffery entered Nyghtshayd's room he lit a candle waiting for her to wake from her deathly slumber. He watched intently memorizing every detail of her sweet, beautiful heart shaped face. He'd loved her from afar all these years, never dared to admit that to himself until now. He walked to her bed and lovingly caressed her face kneeling beside her for just a moment to kiss her lifeless lips. As he straightened up she stirred, smiled at him as he raised the axe and cut off her head.

He bathed and packed quickly. He went to the stables and saddled his horse; he put a halter on Nyghtshayd's mare and tethered his few belongings to her saddle. There was one last thing to do. He entered the mansion placing a white candle in the kitchen window and lit it. He went up the stairs and threw a match on the kerosene he'd already doused the rooms with, the fire spread quickly. He raced to the cellar steps he lit an oil lamp turning the wick up high and watched it burn before throwing it down into the cellar. He watched for a moment as the cellar burst into flames. He walked through the house to the front door where the horses were tethered. He looked around one last time before lighting another lamp and throwing it into hallway. He ran to the horses leading them safely away from the blazing mansion.

As the midnight hour approached on Samhain a lone rider, with two horses sat upon the hill watching. The moon was full in the dark velvet sky illuminating the meadow below. In the distance the church bell rang out the midnight hour. The man and horses watched in silence as two familiar figures emerged from the charred ruins of Bramble Wood manor. Tears streamed down the lone riders face as the man and woman hugged then strolled off into the night hand in hand.

Lightning Source UK Ltd.
Milton Keynes UK
UKHW010447070223
416581UK00014B/648/J